Red Queen Series,

Book 2:

Strike of the Viper

By Dan Donoghue

Red Queen Series, Book 2: Strike of the Viper

Writers Exchange E-Publishing
PO Box 372
ATHERTON QLD 4883

Cover Art by: Alinda

Published by Writers Exchange E-Publishing
http://www.writers-exchange.com

Contents

Chapter 1

Warning

Alaine, Princess of Baden Wood, newly Princess of Vale-of-the-Wood, and soon to become Queen of all Elfdom, lay back in the bath, arched her hips upward, and contemplated the slight roundness of her stomach where it protruded above the soap bubbles. She poked at its gleaming white expanse experimentally a couple of times, then cupped her hands and lifted the warm scented water in a childlike gesture to let it run over her breasts, and ripple down over that interesting bulge. She was pretty sure she was pregnant. She pressed her breasts. She was sure they were firmer, and there could be no doubting the tenderness that had been growing over the last few days, and she suspected the areolas were darkening. It was time to consult with her old nurse.

She sighed, and slid further down in the bath. She was reluctant to face the flurry of fussing that would surely occur as soon as her condition became known. She felt she had just recovered from that which had preceded her wedding, even though three full months had passed since then.

She smiled happily as her mind wandered back over that momentous event. After the terrible experience of her capture by the Nasdarks, and her miraculous rescue by Fairien and his strange companions, her fiancé had been very reluctant to let her out of his sight. Even though he was not fully recovered from the terrible wounds he had received in the rescue attempt, and the long suffering of their subsequent flight from the Nasdarks, he had insisted that the wedding be brought forward to the earliest possible date. There were those who claimed that he was not yet strong enough to step into his father's shoes. Her smile widened into a mischievous grin, as she realised how the news of her pregnancy so soon after the wedding would confound those carpers.

Her joy faded, however, as a picture of Dana came into her mind. She remembered, with horror, the agony of watching the Nasdarks make a theatrical display of Dana's rape - slowly stripping the clothes from her body, throwing the pieces into the shrieking crowd where they were fought over as trophies, parading Dana's nakedness, then tying her to the terrible wooden platform, where she struggled as she was mercilessly raped, time after time, while the crowd roared out the count of each ravager's successful violation until he could hold an erection no longer, and staggered away to make place for the next.

That Dana had recovered from that ordeal was almost as miraculous as Alaine's own rescue from a similar fate. How incredibly lucky she had been to be able to lovingly surrender her virginity in the adoring arms of her husband on her wedding night. Poor Dana, loved beyond belief by the strange Giant though she must be, could never experience that.

Alaine fell to wondering where Dana was. She had heard countless stories of the battle before the walls of Mandanna, and of the now legendary King's Hundred, and their exploits under the leadership of the Giant. Her friends in the Sisterhood spoke in awe of the healing powers that Dana could achieve when she coupled in some way with the mind of the Giant, but no words could convey that bathing in love that had occurred sometime in the healing process at Mandanna. Many had tried to tell her of it, but none had found words to describe it. She had often secretly mourned her lack of mind ability even though it would have precluded her from her station as Princess, and certainly as Queen. Now she knew that she had missed something wonderful, and could not help feeling twinges of jealousy as even lowly kitchen maids went into raptures bordering on hysteria at the slightest mention of it.

She had worked hard to get permission to invite Dana to bring her companions, and to return to live with the Elves, and had succeeded, only to find the three disappeared. Only the King at Mandanna, and a few of his most trusted advisers knew where they had gone, and no word was forthcoming even to Fairein. It seemed that the Giant's quest was not yet complete, and he, and Dana, and the strange Drark creature, were still following it. For a few moments, Alaine contemplated the life of high adventure, of seeing strange places and peoples, of danger and battle, that she felt sure Dana must be experiencing, and felt another momentary pang of envy.

It soon passed, however. Safety, and luxury, and a doting husband were definitely preferable, she told herself.

She was just settling back into the warm embrace of the water when a sudden squalling from the neighbouring bathroom shattered her peace. She sat upright with an exasperated sigh. It was that wild child again.

For a few minutes, she tried to ignore the noise and scuffling, made more noticeable by the obvious attempts, by at least one side of the fracas, to minimise it. At last she could stand it no longer. She hit the hand bell that brought her maids running with towels and robe, and, with their help, climbed precipitously out of the water. Hardly waiting to be dried, she shrugged into a robe, and stormed, unannounced, into the offending room. A picture of chaos met her eyes. Three maids and two serving girls struggled to contain the wild creature in the large tub. Amid stifled curses, wildly threshing arms and legs, and cascades of water, they tried to hold and scrub.

"Enough!"

At the barked command the combatants fell apart. The five stood back ringing the tub, trying to show proper respect for their princess, while keeping a wary eye on the one in the tub, who had sprung to her feet immediately she was released, and seemed about to spring from the water, if not from the room itself no matter that she was all wet, soapy, and unclothed. Alaine stood staring at her, a deep frown of annoyance, and puzzlement, marring the beauty of her features. What she saw was a girl, or young woman, of indefinite age. She was elfin in appearance and in the tall, slimness of her figure, but somehow not elfin also. Her face became beautiful as it relaxed from the savage snarl it had been wearing, into an expression of welcome and relief. This expression only added to Alaine's puzzlement. Why did the child-girl-woman submit so readily to control by her, and her husband, and, seemingly, by no one else? Surely, it could not be that she recognised royalty or regal bearing, as her flattering advisers claimed, and yet, from the first day the soldiers had brought her, bound and struggling, into the palace, she had quieted immediately she, or Fairein, had gone near her. With a tiny shake of her head, she thrust the puzzle aside, and turned her attention back to the girl. That, too, represented a puzzle. Her hair was blond bordering on ginger, and now that it had been cut and combed, could be the hair of about ten percent of Elf women. Her face was oval, and rather long, but finely featured, with beautiful even teeth, and lips fuller than most Elfin. Her neck was long, and slender, which was very elfin, and her young breasts were small, and pointed, as were most Elf girls'. Her waist was thin, and her hips swelled in lovely curves above long, slim legs that would be the envy of many an elfin maid. The legs, in themselves, were no minor part of the puzzle. The skin on them was almost unblemished and silky, now that the dirt had been removed, and yet they were supposed to be those of a person who was found running wild in the grasslands of the south, living with wolves, and hunting like one. It just didn't make sense. It was something Alaine would have to go further into when there was time. At the moment it sufficed for her to go forward, take the child's hand, and calm her. She could not but recognise the simple trust that shone in those beautiful blue eyes, as she coaxed the child to sit in the water, and submit to the administrations of the relieved maids.

In a short time they had her washed, dried, combed, and clothed, and, while Alaine held her hand and talked to her, she made no protest, and even seemed to enjoy the attention. It took the combined efforts of the three maids and a burly guard to take her away, however.

Alaine walked slowly back to her rooms still puzzling over the strange girl. She had questioned the soldiers long and exhaustively, but they could give her very little information. Fairein's own horse herders had reported sightings of the girl some time previously, but the reports had gone mostly ignored while the nation's attention had been centred on the wedding of Fairein and Alaine. Then someone had sent soldiers to investigate, and the girl could not be found. Eventually another sighting had led to an expedition that had located her, seemingly living with a pack of wolves, which had apparently fought savagely against mounted soldiers to protect her. She had been captured, dirty, naked, unable to speak except for growls, and snarls, and other wolf sounds, and been bound and brought to the palace. Since then she had caused havoc, except when she was with either Fairein or Alaine. Then she was quiet and amenable, even anxious to please, if one could attribute such a quality, to what was, to all extents and purposes, a wild beast.

Fairein had been, at first, ill-at-ease in her company, but her child-like trust in him, and willingness to do anything he asked, once he managed to convey his wishes to her, soon won him over. She followed him about in an unobtrusive manner, much like a well-trained dog, whenever she was allowed, and, while he was with her, she even made an obvious effort to learn.

He jokingly claimed that she recognised him as leader of the wolf pack, and it was his duty to teach her.

Alaine had not been so successful in teaching her anything, but, at times, she had sat holding her hand, while her tutors had tried, and they declared that just keeping her still, and attentive, was a marvellous aid. More than that, there was little information to work on. Fairein had instructed his herders to find out all they could, and apart from that, they could only hope that the child was intelligent enough to be taught to speak, and so tell her own story. At night she was locked in her room, not only to keep her from escaping and rejoining the wolves, but to protect her from many of the servants who regarded her with something close to dread, believing she was the child of a witch, or even a witch in child guise, with intent to bring harm to the palace.

Alaine was about to retire to her rooms when the clip, clip of hurrying footsteps caught her attention. It was a sound not common in that place, and at that time. It caused her to pause and wait. "Someone's coming," she said in answer to her maids' looks of enquiry. "Wait a moment."

They stood in a little knot outside the door of the bathroom. They did not have long to wait. Olvar, Fairein's personal guard commander, strode into view trailing an ineffectually protesting retinue of Alaine's servants. They all came to an abrupt halt as the commander caught sight of his princess, somewhat inadequately clothed in a damp bathrobe. He reddened and bowed deeply.

"Please accept my apologies for disturbing you in this manner, Princess, but my errand is urgent. I come from Fairein."

Alaine showed her surprise. "And what errand is so important that my husband cannot deliver it himself, and must send you on a servant's task to my private rooms, my Lord Olvar?" She was both puzzled and annoyed.

Olvar glanced briefly at the bevy of servants then bowed again. "Fairein begs you to accompany me to the council rooms, My Lady," he said. "Something strange has occurred which requires your attention."

"At this time? Cannot it wait until tomorrow?"

"My Lord thinks not, My Lady."

"Why has he sent you? Are we in danger?"

"We do not know, My Lady. Fairein is taking no chances."

"Very well. Allow me time to dress, and I will come."

Olvar turned a bright red, and bowed again. "I'm very sorry, My Lady, but Fairein asked that you come at once, and that you do not move from my sight. I have men waiting to conduct you." He gestured, and Alaine became aware of a squad of heavily armed soldiers waiting at the end of the hall.

"My God! Have we been invaded by Nasdarks?"

"That is what we are guarding against, My Lady."

"You are serious? How can this be?" She took a thicker robe from one of the maids, and shrugged into it while Olvar averted his eyes. "I will come of course, but I cannot believe that we are in danger."

"I share your view, My Lady, but Fairein would rather be certain where Nasdarks are concerned, especially with your safety, My Lady." They had entered the hall, and the guard fell in about them with weapons at the ready.

"Why did Fairein not come himself? Is he hurt?"

"No, not at all, My Lady. He is afraid the prisoner might come to harm if he leaves him."

"You have a Nasdark prisoner?"

"Yes, My Lady."

"By the Firetime! This gets stranger by the moment. Where was he captured?"

"He wasn't, My Lady. He gave himself up. Came right to the palace gates, and knocked like an honest man, and asked for you."

"Asked -" Alaine stopped abruptly, causing the marching guard to stumble about in an unsoldier-like manner. "A Nasdark came, and asked to see me?"

"Yes, My Lady. How he got past the border guards and the city guards, I cannot say. Fairein fears it is part of some attack, but cannot see how such an action would help them. But that is why he wants you immediately. The Nasdark will speak to no one else. Not even the threat of death will turn him."

"Why is he afraid someone will harm the prisoner if he left only for a few minutes? Surely he is more confident in the discipline of his own guard."

"Of course, My Lady. It is the identity of the prisoner that has him worried. You see, it is believed he is the leader of the band that captured you, and if someone tells My Lord's father, he'll surely order him executed on the spot."

For the first time, a tiny thrill of fear coursed through Alaine's body. Her step hesitated. "The guard is alert?"

Olvar barked a brief laugh. "You may be sure to that, My Lady. Not even a mouse could get through now, and they couldn't have got an army in without our knowing."

"Of course. Let us hurry. I am anxious to hear what this murdering rapist has to say before he dies."

Olvar's brows shot up, but he said nothing, only gestured the guard on. In a few minutes they entered the great council chamber. Alaine stopped abruptly as her gaze met that of the prisoner. He stood tall and straight amidst his captors, and met her eyes unflinchingly. As all Nasdark's, his eyes were black, but, unlike any other she had seen, his showed neither hostility nor fear. For a man who must know he was about to die, he seemed remarkably calm. He even bowed slightly.

"Good evening, Princess," he said.

Alaine could not reciprocate. She did not trust her voice, and had difficulty ensuring that she walked steadily to her chair beside Fairein, who greeted her without taking his gaze from the captive. When Alaine was seated, Fairein spoke. "The Lady Alaine is here. Now, why have you come?"

The Nasdark shrugged. "I see the Princess recognises me. I am Lord Kantin. She will know that I have considerable standing with my people, and am not some outcast whose word is to be mistrusted." He paused.

Fairein turned to Alaine, an enquiry in his eyes. She nodded. "This is the leader of the band that captured me," she managed, though her voice jumped.

The Nasdark bowed as though she had paid him some compliment. "I have come to bring you warning," he said. He paused as a ripple of derisive laughter ran through the room.

Fairein frowned deeply. "Warning of what?"

"Your women are in grave danger, Prince."

"Our women?"

"Yes. The Red Queen wants them all dead, and she is to be feared, believe me."

"Who is the Red Queen? Why does she seek to harm us? And why do you, of all people, come to us? Surely you must know that you will not leave here alive?"

"Of the first, I cannot tell you. I do not know who the Red Queen is. But you know of the Red Queen Demons of the battle of Mandanna, and how that battle would have been lost, and the King slain in the first ten minutes, if it had not been for the Giant and Drark. They were off their horses, and helpless on the ground ready to be killed, then they were up again, and fighting. The Giant, Drark, and your Lady Companion, Princess, had something to do with that. I do not know how, but the Red Queen was defeated, and she apparently blames Elf Women for it. She fears the mind power of Elfkind, and is plotting to have all destroyed."

"How know you of this?" Fairein broke in.

"As I said, I am, or was, a Captain of a strike force. I gained promotion to War Lord by capturing you, and your ladies, Princess. When I returned from Mandanna, I was in disgrace as one who returns from a lost battle, but I had wounds severe enough to save me from being branded coward. I have been admitted to the Council of War Lords. We have been ordered to rebuild the strength of our forces to strike into your lands, Prince, and our aim is to kill all female Elves of any age." He paused and waited quietly as the cries of outrage circled the hall, and swords were drawn and brandished. Only Fairein's stern command stopped him from being slain on the spot.

"Why do you come to us?"

"I fought in the battle of Mandanna. I was wounded. Wounded so badly that I was dying. I have no doubt about that. Then the Lady, I do not know her name-"

"Dana." Alaine said curtly.

"And then the Lady Dana saved my life."

"You do this in return for the saving of your life?"

"No. My life is of little importance. No. I do this because she saved my life, knowing that I captured her, raped her, caused her great suffering. But there is something else I cannot explain. While she was healing me, I felt such an outpouring of love--not directed at me of course--but I became part of it." He stopped and shrugged. "It affected me greatly."

There was silence. Alaine felt she could hear the breathing of those around her. Fairein stared at the Nasdark, who stood quietly. The guard fingered their weapons. At last, Fairein stirred.

"When will you attack?"

"We do not know. We are to await the Red Queen's command. I'm afraid you will have many more enemies than Nasdarks when the time comes."

"More?"

"All the Red Queen commands. That is all the Black Nations and others south of you. We have been led to believe that there will be no chance of failure. We have been promised your lands as reward, and your men as slaves, but no women are to be allowed to live."

"How are these commands brought to you?" It was Alaine who asked.

The Nasdark turned to her. He looked genuinely puzzled. "I do not know, Princess. I have often wondered. The King appears to know what the Red Queen wishes, but very few seem to know how. There must be a very good spy system organised, as the King seemed to know all about Donwin's troop movements, and numbers, though we saw no messages coming or going. The only thing he didn't know about was the Giant and his party. I would not like to be any of them should the Red Queen find them."

There was a general murmur of agreement. Alaine spoke, her voice now composed. "I still do not understand why you have come to warn us. That you were affected by Dana's action in the circumstances, I can understand, but this seems to me to go beyond gratitude - beyond love even. You have turned traitor against your King and people. Surely your family will suffer horribly. Even if we do not behead you, you will never be able to return to your home, to your friends, family."

The Nasdark smiled grimly up at her. "I have no family to mourn me, or to bear the blame for my actions, Princess. As far as my friends go, they believe me attempting to find another unguarded pass into your lands, and will honour me as killed in the attempt. As for being a traitor to my King, I do not believe I am. I believe the King is not merely allied to the Red Queen. I believe she controls him. I believe she rules the Nasdarks, and I have sworn no allegiance to her, whoever she may be."

"How can that be so? How could the Red Queen get access to your King? And what about the Warlords? We have always believed that the Warlords were almost as powerful as your king."

"That is true, Princess, but some time back the King took a new concubine. She is a white woman. Where she came from no one seems to know. At one time I thought she was the Red Queen. Now I think she is an agent of the Red Queen. I think she has brought our King under her control. Likewise, the very greatest of our Warlords seem also to be controlled. When the King ordered us to muster against Donwin, there were many lesser

Warlords such as myself, who held that we should stay with our traditions, and not become involved in the affairs of others. We held that we should maintain our strength to guard against your revenge, Prince. There were two very powerful lords, whom we expected to support us, as that had always been their position. They surprised us. They supported the King without the slightest objection. They, too, seemed to know more about Donwin than we could understand. They did not know enough, however. Now we have weakened our nation, and gained a terrible foe on our Northern borders. No, Princess, I may be mistaken. I hope very much that I am mistaken, but I fear that Nasdarks do not rule themselves. They have become servants of a stranger."

Fairein stirred. "It grows late," he said. "You will be held until we decide what to do with you." He nodded to the guard who closed about their prisoner.

"No! Hold!" Alaine cried starting to her feet. "My Lord, I would speak on this."

Fairein looked surprised, but gestured hold. "It is late, Princess, cannot this wait the night?"

"No, I think not. Do you believe what he has told you?"

Fairein frowned. "I think so. It has the sound of truth, and naught else makes sense."

"In that case, this man has done us a very great service, My Lord. It is true he has also done us very great wrong, but the one to whom he has done most wrong is Dana, and she has obviously forgiven him. I fear if his case is put to council, he will be condemned without proper consideration." She turned to the Nasdark. "If we set you free, what will you do? You cannot return home."

The captive smiled at her. "I have not made plans, Princess, for fairly obvious reasons. It is true I cannot return home. I am outcast, and will be condemned by my people once they know I still live. If I were to live, I think

I would seek this Queen who has subverted my King, and, if possible, destroy her."

Alaine turned back to Fairein. "I ask that this Nasdark be allowed to live, and to be escorted from our lands. I believe what he said is true, that, if we survive this threat, we will owe that survival to him in great measure. For that service, I ask that he be pardoned his previous harm, especially in light of Dana's actions."

Fairein looked round his councillors. He saw indecision in most eyes. Alaine saw indecision in his. She leaned closer. "For Dana," she whispered.

Fairein straightened. "Women sometimes see things more clearly than we, especially where compassion is concerned." He bowed to her. "It shall be as you ask." He turned back to the Nasdark. "You have been saved a second time by an Elf Lady, Nasdark. It must mean something. Go you in peace. My Strike Commander will see that you have escort to any of our borders you choose. You will be given horse and rations, and your weapons will be returned to you at the border. I wish you well should you find this Red Queen."

The Nasdark bowed. He looked once more at Alaine and bowed his thanks, and then turned with his guard, and they marched out. Olvar followed. Fairein glanced at Alaine. "I hope no one runs with this story to my father. I doubt he'll see the justice in allowing a Nasdark, such as he, to go free."

She smiled. "I think I may have news that will turn his anger and his attention. That Nasdark is a cruel beast, but he is brave and resourceful. He may yet serve us very well indeed by destroying this accursed Red Queen. He is an enemy she does not know, and one she will not expect. He may succeed where Dana and the Giant fail, for she will surely be on her guard against them."

Fairein yawned, and nodded. "As always, my darling, you are, no doubt, right. But at the moment I am too tired to worry about that over much. I fear we have a very difficult and dangerous time ahead. Let us sleep so we'll have clear heads to start the morrow. I wish my father wasn't so ill. His council would be beyond value. What is the news you think he'll welcome so greatly?"

She grinned impishly. "I think I can promise him a grandchild before the year is out."

Fairein stopped abruptly, and swung to face her, his face lighting up with delight. "You mean that? You're pregnant? Are you sure?"

"Reasonably," she managed as he swung her into his arms. "But if you squeeze me too hard, I might cease to be," she gasped.

Fairein was instantly remorseful, and carefully set her on her feet. "Are you alright?"

"Of course, Silly. It takes more than that to hurt a new Prince of the Realm."

"Prince of the Realm." Fairein echoed. "God! If only we didn't have this new peril hanging over our heads. How happy I would be."

Alaine kissed him tenderly. "Be happy, my darling. We have faced perils before. At least, we are warned. It could have been much worse."

"Yes. I must call a meet tomorrow. Let us forget the world tonight, and make love before the women claim you from me."

Chapter 2

Weapon of Fire

"**B**y the Firetime! There's something wrong! Very wrong! Look you there!" The white-clothed captain, his voice sharp with anxiety, indicated the distant tower with a flick of his hand as he conned his vessel into the small, hidden harbour in the far south of the mysterious island of Tasmanka, bringing the ancient tower of the Rulers into view from behind the coastal hills.

The Giant who stood beside him, balancing lightly on the balls of his feet against the slight roll of the vessel, peered at the indicated tower, which seemed to float above the morning mists. "Why?"

"The call flag's up. I haven't seen that used in years. They run that up to summon the men when there's trouble brewing. It used to be used when they were expecting attack from the Ferals."

"Ferals?"

"The Wild Ones. We've had our problems, too, you know. For a long time, after the Firetime, there were two groups here on the island - the Ferals, and us. The Ferals think that all Beforetime things are evil, and want to destroy any that's left, so the Firetime can't come again. Our lot want them preserved for the sake of the great stores of knowledge they represent. We hold that the knowledge, in itself, isn't evil. It is only the purposes that evil men put it to that is. We, or at least out ancestors, were not able to use any of the weapons against the Ferals, of course, as their own people would have torn them to pieces as soon as they were seen even handling the things. There was a lot of strife, but, eventually, we won, in that the Ferals are all but wiped out. You could say that they won, too, because they gave us so much trouble that no one could spend the time studying the things, and then everyone was too busy just getting enough to eat. By the time the famines were over, all the old people who had learned a bit about them were dead. The rulers still talk of setting up things they call Universities to rediscover the knowledge, but nothing ever gets done."

"Why?"

"Don't know. I just run this ship. That's enough for me. There's even stuff on board here that I don't know how to work, or even what it's supposed to do."

All conversation ceased as the ship neared the primitive pier that jutted out some fifty metres from the shore, and sailors rushed to carry out tasks associated with docking. The Drark and Dana came up from below to join the Giant. "It might be best to wear mail when we go ashore," the Giant told them. "The Captain says yon flag means something is amiss."

"Has he any idea what it is?" Dana asked, eyeing the banner balefully.

"Not that he's saying."

"Well. We'll soon find out. There are horses coming. We'd better get into mail if you think it wise."

They hurried below to unpack mail, and tighten it about their bodies, groaning at the loss of comfort and freedom of movement as they did so.

When they returned on deck, horses were waiting for them on the shore, with an escort of twenty armed men. Even the soldiers were clad in the universal white suits. One soldier stepped forward and identified himself as an officer, though he carried no badge of rank. "I have orders to escort you to the Rulers as fast as possible," he announced.

"What has happened?" the giant asked, as he waved farewell to the sailors lined up along the side of the ship, and led the others to the horses.

"I was not told," the officer answered readily enough. "Something is going on in the Tower, but no one is saying what. There's rumours aplenty, but no facts. There's been a complete call of men, and only women are left to get the crops in even with the weather likely to change, so they must think it's pretty important." His expression was one of doubt, however.

They rode at a brisk canter to the tower. As they neared, men could be seen milling around idly to either side of the great doors, or camped in the ruined buildings. It was impossible to tell how many there were. All appeared to be armed with bows, swords, or lances, but they still looked more like disgruntled farmers than soldiers, and discontent could be plainly read on many of the faces. The doors opened at their approach, and they rode through into the interior court. Servants of the Rulers were waiting to conduct them immediately into a large conference room.

The Rulers were seated, waiting. In the centre was the old woman who had been their first contact. On either side, were ranged her colleagues. There were more than they had seen on their first visit, and those on the outer fringes of the group were younger. It seemed promotion came with age in this society. The Giant glanced quickly along the line. The one who had been victim of the Red Queen was not present.

He bowed before them. "We have returned as we promised," he said.

"Greetings and welcome. It is heartening to find people of honour in our troubled times. I hope all is well in your homelands?"

"Our lands have suffered war, Lady. Our enemies were defeated, but with great loss of life, and damage to property. It cannot said to be well, but it could have been much worse. What is the problem in this land that calls for armed men outside your doors, and harvests waiting in the fields?"

"Our problem may well be your own, Giant. Know you, that, some days ago, the Lady Vondue, she who was responsible for the loss of the relic that troubled you, was found foully murdered in her bed. At the same time, we found one of our male Rulers vanished, and with him the serving girl with whom he was romantically attached. At first we thought them also victims of the murderer, but we now have reason to think them likely to be the perpetrators of the deed, as they were seen leaving the building, and two more relics have disappeared."

"What sort of relics are these, Lady?" asked the Giant.

"Weapons. If they can be made to work, horrible weapons of the Firetime."

"What sort of weapons? What do they do?"

"We do not know for sure. We have sought to find out. As far as we can tell, they create something very like lightning, which can be directed at one's enemies to destroy even the strongest buildings - even stone itself, if the writing is true."

The Giant said nothing. A mental picture of such a weapon in the hands of men like the Red Queen Demons robbed him of speech.

"Have they been able to leave the island?" It was Dana who asked.

"There is a boat missing. A ruler such as Bernard could order such a thing and no one would question it."

"Why would he do this thing?"

"We believe that the serving girl is the agent of the Red Queen, who has managed to enslave both the Lady Vondue and Bernard. You went through such an experience, Giant. How do you think it was done in your case?"

The Giant glanced at Dana and grimaced, but answered readily. "When we were with a people called the Femins, a warlike race of women warriors, their ruler believed that her people were suffering from inbreeding, and ordered that a warrior should attend both Pen and my beds each night. Most looked upon it as a simple duty, and approached it, as far as I could tell, as they did all duties, but one had a much more enthusiastic approach. She was very demanding and very seductive. I became very tired, and slept very soundly. A couple of nights later, she took the place of a reluctant warrior, and brought wine. It was after those two nights that I began to lust after the warriors, and I believe that it was while I was in an exhausted sleep that she somehow whispered poison into my mind."

"So, we believed Bernard was seduced, and he, in turn, arranged for the Lady Vondue to be infected, for she was a dear friend of his. He must be completely under the control of this woman to murder one he loved at her bidding."

"How long have they gone?" It was the ever-practical Drark who asked.

"The boat left with the morning tide two days ago."

"Have you any idea where they are headed?"

"None. They could have gone anywhere. We had hopes that you might be able to help us. You know more of this Red Queen than any of us."

"We know little enough, Lady. In the land of the Snake People she seemed most known. We feel that her Stronghold is close by."

"You have travelled that land. If you wished to get the weapons there, how would you do it?"

"Either in the wagons of a merchant or travelling entertainers. These could pass through Fenderland with little difficulty. Then, once near the Firetime Sands, they could disappear into it, and no one would know where they went. They would have trouble on the other side, however, for they would have to get past the Femins, and that would be no easy task. There are no free merchant caravans, or entertainers, travelling that grim country."

"You, however, have evidence that there are agents of the Red Queen in the land of the Femins."

"That is true," the Giant stated grimly. "I would meet this twister of minds again. Be she woman or no."

"She may carry your child, Giant," Dana stated just as grimly.

The Giant stared at her. "May the Firetime come again, if she does!" he swore, and all there could see he was visibly shaken by the thought.

"This gets us nowhere," the leader of the Rulers broke in. "We have all the boats we can spare, and people who know a little of Fenderland, out trying to trace where they might have landed. We have our entire man-power called and waiting. It is time we acted. While we are talking, those weapons are moving away from us. Will you lead our men in search of them?"

"We will search for them, Lady. We have more need to find them than you have, but we will be better without others. Too many people attract too much attention. If your men can find a trace of them, then we will follow it. If they have this weapon working when we find them, then only stealth, and surprise attack, will win through. Send your men back to their fields. Find us horses that can carry us, and we will do what we can. It seems that your Ferals may have been right, Lady. These things should have been destroyed long ago."

Some murmurs of agreement or dissent greeted this speech, but nothing came of it. It seemed a very short time, and the three were back on-board ship with horses and gear loaded, and standing off shore, so that they might not be held up for want of a tide when news came through. Pigeons would carry the news to the Tower, and a small boat would bring it to the ship. So, they waited.

Two days passed. The Giant fretted at the delay, pacing the deck like a caged animal. Dana sat, more composed, but anxiously scanning the horizon from time to time. The Drark smoked his pipe and waited, in all outward appearance, completely oblivious of the urgency of their mission.

When news came, it did so with shocking suddenness. Two boats hove in sight, fully rigged, and running before a stiff breeze. One continued on towards the island; the other swung out to stand off them. A small boat was lowered, and fought its way across the buffeting waves to bring up against the side of their craft. A short, weather-beaten sailor clambered aboard with cat-like agility.

The three watched while he spoke rapidly to their captain. The newcomer waved his hands about a lot and spat overboard a number of times. Then, after a curious stare at them, he swung back over the rail, and down into his boat, which shoved off immediately, and went rocking away on the seas. The three joined the Captain who was standing, watching the little boat grimly.

"What news?" asked the Giant with barely contained impatience.

"Bad!" was the reply. "Yon was the boat that the ruler Bernard took. They found it floundering at sea. The crew are missing, and the Ruler, Bernard, mad. He was alive when they came upon him, but screamed at them, and tried to prevent them from boarding. When he couldn't stop them, he jumped overboard, and swam away from the boat, and, though they tried to rescue him, he avoided their efforts, and eventually drowned."

"Were the woman and the weapons still on board?" the Giant asked anxiously.

"No. There was no sign of them. They have most likely been landed."

"What now?" Dana asked. "What happened? Could the crew have gone ashore for some reason and been marooned by Bernard?"

"It is possible," answered the Giant, "but it is more likely they landed, and met up with others who murdered the crew, took the weapons and the woman, and either didn't care enough to murder Bernard, or allowed him to escape. Either way, it probably didn't matter a lot to them. In fact, these Red Queenists would probably enjoy letting him live to suffer longer."

Dana shuddered. "Can they all be so evil? Did that man have any idea where they might have landed?"

The Captain nodded. "From the wind and the currents, Drant thinks she might have come off Grave Yard Point. It's an isolated stretch of coastline to the North West. It would be an ideal place to wait in secret. There's the remains of a Beforetime cemetery there. Not much left really, but the place has a bad name, and people avoid it. Rumour has it, that people staying too long near there get sick and die for no apparent reason."

"Let's hope the Red Queenists were waiting there a long time then," the Giant growled. "Can you land us there?"

"In twelve hours, if the wind keeps up." He left and began calling orders.

Dana, the Giant, and the Drark went below as the ship began heeling as she tacked into the wind.

***

Once more the three were alone. They stood beside their horses on a windswept, desolate shore with the raucous calls of seagulls competing with the crash of breakers, and with the slashing of the wind robbing them of effective speech. They waited as the ship, running before the wind, rapidly dwindled into a tossing toy, and disappeared into the gathering mists. Then they turned as one and led the horses up over the dunes, across a shimmering lake of Firetime glass, and through the sad rows of ancient, crumbling headstones.

They travelled for some time through the desolation until they reached a small stream of flowing sweet water. There, the Giant and Dana set up camp while the Drark went off in search of signs that others might have travelled that way. He returned, just on dark, to report that another camp had been used about a half-hour's walk away on the same stream, but the wind had destroyed most of the signs. There had been at least ten, and possibly twice that number, of shod horses drinking at the stream.

"Ten to fifteen men with pack horses," the Giant said.

"Probably less if they wanted to travel fast." The Drark answered.

"Those travelling fast will attract attention. They'll have to slow down when they reach settled areas, unless they're disguised as soldiers or something," Dana said.

"A risky thing to do," the Drark observed. "I still think merchants or entertainers. We need to find Glendeeshon or his son."

"Is there any clue as to which way those campers travelled?" the giant asked.

"None that I could find. The sand is moving with the wind. We could search for days and find nothing."

"Then tomorrow we ride for Tander. Let us hope that Glendeeshon is at home, or near it."

There was little to hinder them on their way. They had been well supplied with Fenderland coin by the Tasmankans, and could pay for lodgings and meals. The ease and speed with which they travelled brought no comfort to their minds however, as it only added to the worry that their quarry was travelling just as easily, and with like speed.

At every town and village where they stopped, they asked for news of merchants' caravans, or travelling entertainers. At first, they were heartened to hear of a merchant selling mainly kitchenware, and buying scrap steel. Because a load of scrap steel would make an excellent hiding place for the weapons, they went out of their way to track it down, only to find it composed of five decrepit wagons run by a couple of old men and their sons, and headed home in the south. The three had lost almost a full day. Then, as they neared more populated areas, they were overwhelmed with accounts of merchants and entertainers. It was well into autumn. The crops were all harvested. It had been a good year. There was money in people's pockets, and they were in a mood to enjoy themselves before the hard days of winter settled over them. There were merchants and entertainers everywhere. There was little the three could do but ride as fast as possible to Tander.

The first of the winter storms caught them before they reached the city. They were held up for two anxious days in a dismal wayside inn by an early blizzard, and were forced to suffer their host's interminable tales of the people who had visited his establishment, and of past storms, which had cut the roads for weeks. Dana and the Giant escaped as much as possible, while the Drark smoked his pipe, and listened with calm patience.

They were tired and dispirited when they at last clattered up to Glendeeshon's front door. Luck smiled on them, at least to the extent that he had just returned home for the winter. He and his wife welcomed them with heartening enthusiasm, and Randeeshon and Melinda were immediately sent for.

Melinda came in, shyly beautiful, and big with child, and rushed with a glad cry into Dana's arms. Randeeshon stood grinning, foolishly proud, as his wife's condition was the subject of general comment. For a while, they could forget their fears and worries in good fellowship and reunion.

That night, however, as they sat before a fire, and sipped the merchant's wine, their purpose could no longer be deferred, and the Giant outlined their new quest.

Melinda was again questioned closely on her knowledge of the Red Queen, but she could add no more than she had told before. The Red Queen was often referred to in her home. No one, however, seemed to know just who, or what, she was, and no one had ever claimed to have met her. The priests of Sturk had started to speak of her, more and more, in their harangues of the people, and they had become to know more of what the people were doing. It was as though their spies had suddenly become far more effective, and it was generally thought that the Red Queen was supplying them with information. When Melinda was young, she remembered, there had been people who had opposed the use of snakes and of poison, but as she grew up, these had disappeared, and fear had grown more in the community. Her father was a powerful warlord who still held such views, though he no longer expressed them. That, and her instinctive dislike of the priests of Sturk, was mainly why she had refused, when invited to become a handmaiden of Sturk, and had almost lost her life because of it.

Glendeeshon could offer little advice. He agreed that a merchant's caravan, or a troupe of entertainers, would be the best way to get such dangerous relics across the country. He felt that the merchant's caravan would be the best option, as anyone could pretend to be a merchant if he didn't mind losing money, and he had been supplied with merchandise, whereas entertainers were expected to be able to entertain wherever they stopped, and would incur suspicion if they did not do so. He felt that their best course was to hurry to the land of Small Ones, and ask after any strangers passing through their country. It would, however, be necessary to have someone in the party whom the Small Ones trusted, and it was agreed that Randeeshon would accompany them even though he might get snowbound for the winter, and miss the birth of his child.

That decided, there was little else to do except try to satisfy Glendeeshon's unquenchable thirst for knowledge of lands and people. The Femins, in particular, fascinated him, and, despite the Giant's emphatic warnings of the danger in approaching such fierce warriors, he extracted a promise that, should the strife with the Red Queen be brought to a successful conclusion, the Giant would ask permission of the Femins that he should be allowed to take a caravan into their lands. Melinda agreed to give them a message to her father in the hope that he might be prevailed upon to aid them, should they be forced to attempt another crossing of that fearful domain. It was felt too dangerous to address it directly to him in case it fell into the hands of the priests, but she remembered a childhood sobriquet that he would recognise, and which would prove to him that the message came willingly from her hand.

As on the southward journey so many months ago, the merchant's renown eased their way across the miles of Fenderland. The weather was their greatest foe, but, at least, they had the comfort of knowing that it was impartial, and gave just as much trouble to their quarry as to themselves. As they travelled northward, the weather became more kind. The land became drier, and the blizzards of the south merely scattered a thin coating of snow across their path. The tales of merchant caravans and entertainers became markedly less, as all such hurried to their various winter quarters. They began to hear of a group hurrying ahead of them, but it was composed of only one wagon, and five or six, riders. Their most reliable informant stated that there were three women travelling in the wagon, and five men riding escort. They seemed to be keeping to back-roads, and avoiding soldiers, or, at least, soldiers on duty. He said the latter with a smirk that alerted the Drark.

"Why is that?" He asked.

The informant glanced briefly at Dana, and positively leered. He was fortunately unaware of how close he came to having the Giant's fist descend upon his head. It seemed the ladies danced in very revealing costumes in the less respectable inns at night for a little money, and then made a lot of money entertaining the local men in their rooms during the rest of the night. It was a custom frowned upon by the authorities mainly because of the health problems associated with such activity, but the soldiers, when off duty, preferred to take advantage of the ladies' charms, as opposed, to hauling them off to the local magistrates. They could generally be prevailed upon to let the ladies know where those on duty would not be next day.

"Do you think these prostitutes are worth considering?" Dana asked, when they were alone again.

"I don't think so," the Giant replied. "There's not enough men with them if we were right about the camp on the shore. These are probably an unfortunate group of entertainers who fell out with their fellows, and are trying to make enough to carry them over winter."

The Drark nodded. "It is strange though. When we were caught in the inn during that blizzard we had, the inn keeper spoke of a group such as this, only there were four women and four men." He turned to Randeeshon. "Is this common?"

Randeeshon shook his head. "Not very common," he said. "There's not a lot of call for travelling prostitutes. Morals are pretty free in the cities, and there are local brothels with a very closed guild. Any strangers are sent packing very fast - that's why they have to have escorts to protect them - though five men for three women is overdoing it a bit. Out here, in the country, they can do all right if the women are slim and pretty, and so long as they keep moving. It's not the soldiers, so much as the local women, they have to watch out for. Country women have to work hard in the fields, and they soon lose their figures, and their complexions. They resent city women, whom they consider pampered. If word gets ahead that prostitutes are coming, especially if they are suspected of spreading disease, the women will try to ambush the party. If they succeed, the prostitutes are generally mutilated to such an extent that, if they survive at all, they are never able to carry on their trade again. No man will go near them. It's a risky business. If they show any signs of having any disease when the women catch them, they're strung up on the nearest tree. Women can be damned savage, especially against their own kind, when they're let loose." He grinned at Dana, who poked her tongue out at him, and threatened to tell Melinda on him.

"I think we should ignore them and carry on as fast as possible," said the Giant. "We lost time before hunting down possible leads, and if we waste too much time, they'll be into the sands, and it will be damned hard finding anyone in that mess, especially if they know where the water is."

A week later found them camped at the same water hole where they had first met Randeeshon and his father. They waited at the camp, spelling the horses, and sorting equipment, while Randeeshon went amongst the Small Ones seeking news of travellers. He returned, after two days, with the news that a party, fitting the description of the three prostitutes and their escort, had passed through on a little used back road just to the west of them on the day they had made camp. It had greatly puzzled the Small Ones as there was nothing in that direction but the Firetime Sands. They must have been travelling on parallel routes almost in sight of each other. Now their quarry had a two-day start.

They broke camp at once, and with Randeeshon guiding, travelled into the night to reach the place where the wagon had last been seen. For part of the night, luck relented, and a full moon gave them sufficient light to follow the narrow, rutted track that wound through wooded valleys, and crawled and switchbacked, up the sides of hills without any conceivable aim or direction. The new wagon tracks were clearly visible even in moonlight, and the hunters pushed their horses hard to make up time. Then the fates frowned, and a cloud bank swelled up from the south, and obscured the moon, making travel almost impossible. They used the last of the light to find a sheltered place to camp, and settled down for the night.

Morning found them away as soon as it was light enough to see the tracks. The clear skies of the previous days had given way to a clouded gloom, but they were too close to the desert to fear blizzard or rain. A cold wind blew from behind, however, and, every now and then, a faint splattering of snow was flung against their backs. It was bitterly cold. They didn't stop for a midday meal, but delayed only long enough to shift their gear onto spare mounts, and ate hard rations as they rode.

By late afternoon, the track had reached the site of a deserted, and ruined village, then rapidly dwindled into nothing. The wagon tracks continued on for a little way through the dry grass, then struck off due north. There could be no doubt left as to its destination.

Night caught them on the edge of the desert where they made a cheerless, dry, and cold camp. It was decided that Randeeshon could be of no further help. He was not skilled in the use of weapons, and to allow him to continue with them, would only take him needlessly into danger. So they spent some time sorting gear again for a quick dash into the Sands, taking only hard rations, and water, and leaving the rest for Randeeshon to take back with him on his attempt to reach his home before winter closed the roads to him.

In the early hours of the morning, they bade goodbye, and set off once more with weapons ready, and hearts grimly determined. A couple of hours after sunrise they came upon the wagon. It had been pushed over a bank into a dry gully on the edge of the sand country. There was evidence that the party had camped there at least one night, and had also sorted gear. A roll of cloth had been tossed after the wagon. It contained three very brief female costumes glittering with gold and silver thread, and bottles, and vials of perfumes and facial paints. They found other female clothing in the wagon, together with cooking equipment, and even food.

Tracks of about ten horses led into the sands while there was vegetation to shelter them, but as the grass became more sparse, the tracks became less distinct, and, with the wind still blowing from behind carrying sand with it, quickly faded out completely.

"What now?" Dana asked when they could no longer find a trace of a footprint.

"It seems we have no choice but to ride north as fast as possible," said the Giant. "If we come upon them, well and good. If not, we alert the Femins, and seek to stop them there. At least there we go to friends. If they get through into the Snakes, our chances of stopping them are small indeed."

"Then let us go," the Drark growled. "I grow tired of this chasing across the country, and my behind hurts."

"If they have found out how to use that weapon none of us may have behinds to hurt before long," Dana told him as they moved off. "What does it feel like to get hit by lightning, think you?"

"I know of none who have lived to tell, Lady, but I fear it would not be pleasant. Let us hope that the Red Queen is too unsure of her power to give such a potent weapon into the hands of even her own servants. It has been my experience that tyrants fear their closest more than they do their enemies."

"You may be right there, Drark. If she rules by fear, then she might fear to allow her servants to seek to use the weapon. According to the Tasmankans, it is not an easy thing to make to work."

In the afternoon, some days later, flights of birds alerted them to the presence of an oasis before they could see any sign of it. They stopped and rested the horses, then, as darkness closed over the desert, and before the moon rose, they rode as rapidly as possible in the general direction of the oasis, but veering off to the east. When the moon rose they dismounted, and climbed carefully to the top of a dune. They could make out the palms, silver in the distance. For most of the night they continued on, until they had reached a position to the north east of the palms, and separated from them, only by a low dune. There they rested, waiting for the dawn. No firelight came from the silent palms, but no curlews called either, and, every now and then, a faint scent of smoke drifted across to them. As the dawn broke, a horse whinnied, and they held their own horses' muzzles to prevent answer. The spare mounts had been left well back out of earshot.

They held a hurried, whispered conference. It was essential that they took the camp by surprise in case the weapons were operational, and could be used against them. If they were going to do that, they had to be certain that the people there, were, in fact, their quarry. A sudden attack on the most innocent of travellers would be taken as an attack by bandits, and would result in fighting, in which, almost all, would be killed or wounded. The Giant had positioned them so that they could rush the camp with the rising sun at their backs, blinding their opponents. They finally agreed that despite the risk of hurting innocent people, they would have to rush the camp. They lay very still with their heads in scooped out hollows in the sand so that the outline of the ridge would seem unbroken against the glow of dawn, and watched the oasis.

With the light, the camp stirred. A figure broke from the palms, walked to the edge of the water, stripped and waded in. It was a woman. The Giant cursed softly. Another wandered down and dipped water, and called ribald comments about the effect of the cold water on the bather's anatomy, and subsequent love making ability. The sun flooded against their backs. The three wriggled back and mounted. The sunlight hit the tops of the palms, and ran rapidly down their trunks. The Giant gestured, and the three dug spurs to their mounts, and rushed them over the dune, and down onto the solid earth along the edge of the water. They swept past the startled swimmer, and Dana used her boot to knock the second woman to the ground as she ran, shrieking, back towards the palms, where the camp was springing into action.

At the edge of the palms, they met arrows and swords, but their mail stopped the first, and their own swords crashed havoc on the second. They broke through to the tents. A man staggered out with a metal object in his arms that could only be one of the weapons. He struggled as it snared in the folds of the tent for a few fatal seconds, then swung it to point at the Giant.

With a mighty leap, the Giant threw himself from the horse. The whole world seemed to burst into forge glare, and searing heat thrust along his side. He hit the ground, and rolled, coming up with sword held like a lance, and threw himself in a long dive at his enemy. The man was awkwardly trying to bring the muzzle of the weapon down as the Giant flew under it, and his sword drove into the man's chest, crashing up to the hilt in his body. The weapon flared again, but, by then, it was pointed in the opposite direction, and, suddenly, the tent was gone, as were the palms behind it. The Giant rose with the weapon in his left hand, and his bloody sword in the right. Two men rushed at him. One he cut down with his sword, the other he hit with the weapon. Both sprawled in the sand. He spun round seeking other enemies. None showed. The Drark was wiping his sword against the body of a man, and, on catching the Giant's glance, gestured up to the top of one of the palms where another hung in the fronds with an arrow through his throat.

That was four. They both looked anxiously for Dana, and found her quietly riding her horse around the edges of the water keeping the swimmer trapped in the centre. Of the Giant's horse, only a few scraps of charred meat could be found, and the woman, who Dana had knocked down, had been unwise enough to scramble back to her feet. She existed only from the waist down. The Giant went back towards the place where the tents had stood, feeling sick. He was suddenly much sicker. There had been people still in one of the tents. Two by the look of it. So, there must have been at least one more added to the party, probably someone to guide them through the desert, and possibly through the land of the Femins. It might even have been the redheaded warrior who had twisted his mind. It was impossible to tell. They formed a charred conglomerate that seeped blood onto the blackened remnants of a bedroll.

The Drark remounted and set off to check the rest of the oasis. The Giant searched fruitlessly through the wreck of the camp for the second weapon. Some stored gear had escaped the blast, but nothing was large enough to hide a thing as big as the weapon he held. When he was sure it was nowhere near, he walked slowly down to the side of the water, stepping finicky around the half body.

The swimmer was evidently growing tired in the cold water. She trod water turning to watch first Dana, then the Giant, then the palms, saying nothing.

"They're all dead," the Giant growled. "Come on out. You cannot stay there forever."

She did not answer. Her face was strangely calm. She stayed until the Drark came back through the palms leading horses. Then, without a word, she slipped quietly under the surface. The Giant stared amazed, then cursed, and began tearing at the buckles of his mail. Dana urged her mount into the water, and swam it towards the place where the woman had disappeared. The Giant cursed anew, and tore the mail from his body, fearful that Dana would slip from the horse, and, strong swimmer though she was, the mail she wore would surely drag her under. When she reached the place, she rolled off the horse, gripped the saddle with one hand, and pushed herself out, and down, feeling with her feet. After surfacing for breath a couple of times, she managed to snag the woman's body and drag it to the surface. She grabbed hold of the long hair with her free hand, and hauled it across the saddle pulling the head up out of the water. The horse began to struggle towards the shore making poor headway with its double load. The Giant rid himself of his mail at last, and rushed to their aid. He took the limp body and swam with quick strokes to the shore, where the Drark was standing over the weapon, his bow ready in his hands The Drark faced the palms lest there still be enemies, and they with the second fearful weapon.

Dana found bottom, let the horse go, and waded out to them. Together, she and the Giant bent over the woman. She tried to touch the mind with healing but found it gone. She shook her head. "She's dead. She must have deliberately breathed in water to die so quickly."

Together they stared down at the naked body. It was young, barely out of adolescence, almost perfect in shape, and despite death's marks, still breathtakingly beautiful. "This is the one who seduced Lord Bernard, I'll warrant." murmured the Giant.

"She was lovely enough to do it anyway," answered Dana. "What think you, Drark?"

"I have seldom seen such beauty, Lady. It pains me deeply to see it wasted in so sorry a cause."

"The other lady was lovely enough also until the fire hit her," said Dana. "You are lucky you left your horse so swiftly Giant. Your mail would have been of little use against that fire, I think. It was very quick thinking on your part. Most people would have tried to ride him down."

"You forget I seem to know what people are going to do in the heat of battle, Lady. I knew that something terrible was going to happen, though I had no idea how terrible. See you across the water? It has burned through a large part of the dune, and turned the sand to water."

"Not water, Giant," said the Drark. "Glass! Remember this is a Firetime weapon." He bent and picked it up gingerly. "I like it not. It seems to be dead now though. What I'd like to know, is where the other is? Let us not stand here, looking at dead ladies, until we've found it and have it safe."

"Well said, Drark," Dana said. "The very thought of it makes me cold."

They searched through the oasis. Backward and forwards, they searched, all afternoon, only stopping long enough to bury the dead. At last, as night came on, they were forced to admit that the second weapon was not there. No tracks left the oasis. They could only conclude that it had not been brought in. It was the Drark who voiced the thoughts that had been building up in all their minds. "The other wagon the Inn keeper spoke about, the one that had four women and four men, think you, it carried the other weapon, and went a different route?"

"I had thought of it," said the Giant grimly. "I hoped it couldn't be true."

"What now?" Dana asked. "Do we ride for the Femins as we were going to do?"

"I don't like the idea of taking a weapon like this anywhere near the Femins," returned the Giant. "I fear they would try to take it from us. Think what they would do to the Snake People if they got such a thing."

"Would that be so bad?"

"Yes. I think so. Remember, Melinda is of the Snake People. Have we not grown to like her - even love her? There must be many others like her. Would you see them blasted? This weapon kills everyone, even friends, as we've just seen."

"I think it would be futile anyhow," Dana remarked. "This party was headed through the Femins' country. What would be the use of separating, and going different ways through Fenderland where there was little danger, if they meant to come together in Femins' country where there is every danger? I think the others were veering west, and would have gone, by some route, in the Western Mountains. This is probably the most direct, and quickest way, but a mountain route, if they could get into them before winter closed the passes, would be sure. What think you, Drark?"

"You speak with wisdom, Lady. If they know of places in which they can weather storms, and where they have food caches, then they will surely be safe from pursuit by now, and, even if they lose their lives, the Red Queen will probably know where the weapon lies. No doubt one, or more, of these people were able to stay in contact with her through mind power. If I'm not badly mistaken, one was the young lady in the water. That is probably what she was doing while she swam, and, when she had no more to report, she took her own life, or was compelled to do so. I fear the Red Queen will most likely be aware of all that happened here and of our present position. I, too, think it unwise to take this weapon closer to the areas of her strength. We know, only too well, how easily the Snake People can put us to sleep."

"Should we destroy the weapon?" Dana suggested.

The Giant shook his head. "I wish we could, but they warned me in Tasmanka not to attempt to do so. They believe that it could return the Firetime, and destroy us, and all around us, if we did. In fact, the writing suggests these particular weapons were not much used because they could not be trusted fully even by those who made them."

"So, what do we do?"

"There seems but one course. We must take this one back to Tasmanka and report our failure. Then we must wait until winter is over, and go in search of the other. It is possible that the Red Queen seeks to use the weapon only to defend her stronghold. If that is so, when we find her, we'll also find the weapon."

"Not a thing I'm looking forward to particularly," grimaced the Drark.

"Nor I," sighed Dana. "Let us leave this horrible place, and camp in the desert. At least out there the air is clean."

Chapter 3

Seduction

The Giant stood on the crumbling battlements of the ruined tower of the Rulers of the Island of Tasmanka. Beside him stood Endearia, High Ruler of the Island. About them, the last of a late winter blizzard blew itself out in a spiteful hurling of sleet against their backs, and a vicious slashing at their faces. Endearia shivered and drew her cloak closer about her thin body. "Why must you seek so inhospitable an aerie to ponder, Giant? Does warmth and walls so clog your brain? Or do you shun the company of mere mortals?"

"Not so, My Lady. I but fret in closed places, and in those not made for giants, and my bones cry for action whenever I think of the time passing and the Red Queen with that other weapon. We have fought many foes, and bitter ones, since this mad quest started, but none has galled us like this winter. Does God really stand on this Queen's Right Hand? I'm beginning to think He does."

Endearia smiled, and sighed. "I very much doubt it, Peter. Know you, that you are named for one who stood by the right hand of the God of the Beforetime. Peter the Rock, I think he was called. Why 'rock', I don't know.

Perhaps, like most men, he was hard-headed. Anyhow, Peter the Giant is as good a name as Peter the Rock. Come inside. You are worn from hard travel, and it will do no good to have you ill when the winter dies. Besides, I have need to speak with you, and I cannot stand this cold. Age has its disadvantages, too."

They left the half-light of a winter evening for the flickering light of the dank halls, and descended to warmer regions. Dana and the Drark, together with five of the senior Rulers, awaited them. The Giant looked closely at his companions as he took the chair indicated. It was true, he had to admit. The hard winter journey from the Firetime Sands had taken their toll. Dana looked drawn and very tired, and even the Drark slumped in his chair. The Giant was surprised to find how much he, too, welcomed the cushioned comfort of the seat assigned to him.

When they were all seated, and warm wine had been passed round, Endearia opened the discussion. "What now, Giant? What are your plans?"

The Giant sighed. "There is not much choice, Ruler. We are still committed to finding the Red Queen, and the other weapon, but how?... I wish I knew. I do not know whether it would be best to strike straight north for the Vipands or to try to follow the path of the second weapon."

"Is there hope of finding it before it reaches the Red Queen, think you?" one of the other Rulers asked.

The Giant studied him. He had been introduced as Denard but that was all the Giant knew of him. He was short of stature, old, as was all the High Rulers, plump, where most were thin, short sighted, and rapidly going bald. He seemed intelligent and interested. Some of the others sat expressionless and could have been thinking of anything, or not thinking at all.

"If we can get away soon, there is perhaps a chance. The winter has been severe in all parts that we have travelled. There is little doubt that it will have been worse in the Western Mountains. It could be that the party is still snow bound somewhere in there. The Red Queen will, no doubt, send aid to her people as soon as possible, if only to recover the weapon. If we could beat them to it, then it would be far easier to win it back from winter wearied travellers than from her hands, I warrant."

"Would it not be better to make straight for the land of this Red Queen, and try to ambush the weapon party as they bring it in?"

"Perhaps. If we knew just where she reigns. We think she is in the Mountains to the West of the Vipands, but that is far from certain. Melinda knew nothing but rumour of her."

"How can there be a Queen, and no one knows her country? Does she really exist?" It was the Ruler sitting next to Denard who spoke in a thin, petulant voice.

Denard turned to her with a pitying look, and an ever so slight curl of his upper lip. "The Lady Vondue, and Bernard, is proof enough of that, I think," he said. "But what say you, Giant? How is it that everyone seems to have heard of the Red Queen, but no one can say where she dwells?"

"Perhaps she doesn't wish people to know where she is until she is stronger," Dana answered for the Giant. "I think she might not have been born a queen. Perhaps she is just someone who has gained strong mind-powers from the Firetime, and is building an empire."

"A Firetime Throw-out. Perhaps cast out by her people, and seeking revenge on everyone. That could explain the need for the Firetime weapons. If she has few soldiers, she would need strong weapons."

"It does not explain her knowledge of the weapons," the Giant said. "Surely the woman who came and corrupted Lord Bernard, knew what she sought. Such an operation needed resources, and knowledge, far greater than would be in the hands of an outcast. So, too, would the incitement of Mondar to attack Ungar, and the involvement of the Nasdarks, to say nothing of the giants. No. This Queen might rule an unknown country, but she is not without queenly resources."

"So our goals remain the same. We have need to seek her out, and, if possible, destroy her. Are we agreed?" Endearia slowly looked round the room catching the eyes of each in turn.

"Would one need to destroy her? After all, if she is a Queen - I mean could we not seek to come to terms with her - perhaps a treaty or something?" It was a timid looking Ruler who had said nothing before, who spoke. Her voice dropped away as she read the expressions on the faces of her companions.

"I was very fond of Lord Bernard and Lady Vondue," Endearia said grimly. "And by all accounts, this Queen has caused much bloodshed of innocents. I would have all such as she destroyed."

This time, as Endearia looked each in the eyes, she read agreement. "That is settled then. As soon as our men of weather lore proclaim winter's end, you will be ready to travel once more. You will have the best we can offer. God go with you." She rose to indicate that the meeting was at an end.

Far to the north, the winter had already ended except in the very high country of the Elfin Kingdom. Fairein rode with a small group of guardsmen down from an inspection tour of the mountain passes. He had found them well-guarded, the warriors brisk and in good spirits as they waited the onset of spring. Those who guarded against the Nasdarks had always been the elite of the elfin forces. Long years of battle had built proud traditions and spawned countless heroes and heroines. Border guards looked upon the coming summer as a time of testing, in which they might gain great honour, and high promotion. They had fought Nasdarks so often successfully in the passes that they were supremely confident that they could hold against any onslaught. In that, Fairein was inclined to agree. Even dour old Olvar cautiously admitted that he could find little fault with their state of readiness.

The south was a very different matter, however. No one really believed that an attack would come from there. Even decades before, when the border posts had been set up, they were in response to bandit attacks rather than any concern that a southern country might raid against them. The great sand and saltbush plateau seemed to be the end of the world. Those border guard companies had for years been looked upon as places of exile, where troublesome younger sons were shipped to learn some manners and responsibilities, or, at least, to get them out of the way, where they would not cause embarrassment in polite society.

Fairein had been trying to stir them out of comfortable apathy into a state of war readiness, when there was absolutely no signs whatever that anything was any different from that of the last half century. It was almost exactly fifty years since the last bandit raid.

Now, as he rode slowly homewards, he sighed. Improvements were coming frighteningly slowly in the south, and, if that wasn't enough to make him depressed, he had nothing to look forward to at home except an empty, lonely bed. Alaine had been taken from him by a multitude of nurses and midwifes, though she had hardly started to show her pregnancy. He was certainly not let near her. It wasn't for her sake or his, but for the safety of the heir to the Kingdom. Nothing must be done that might jeopardise him. No one seemed to hold the slightest doubt that Alaine was carrying a son. Perversely, Fairein hoped for a girl. But what he wanted most was Alaine in his bed to make love to, to love him, and to reassure him that all would be well. He moved restlessly in the saddle, trying to find a more comfortable seat. His buttocks were sore, and the insides of his thighs were chaffed and blistered. His long illness, and then the preparations for his wedding, and the responsibilities of state due to the illness of his father, had kept him out of the saddle for far too long. He was paying the price now, and was very conscious of the sardonic glances directed at him by Olvar every time he tried to get more comfortable.

He was profoundly happy when the palace came into view through the trees. Alaine was there to greet him, looking even more lovely than he remembered, but when he went to take her in his arms, he found fussing midwifes all around him, as though they expected him to jump upon, and rape, his wife there before them all. Alaine apparently read his thoughts as she always seemed to be able to do, and smiled sadly at him as she was bundled off. He cursed bitterly, and was short in his dismissal of his men, and then angry with himself, as he read, by their amused expressions, that they knew exactly why he was being short with them.

A long, warm, bath, and three equally long, cool glasses of wine did a lot to restore his body, if not his spirits. After he had dressed, there still remained an hour or more before the evening meal would be ready. He went to see if he could find Alaine, but was told that she was in her bath, and asked, in a disapproving manner by an officious head mid-wife, if his errand was important enough to disturb her. He left, vowing that if he were ever allowed near enough to his wife to get her pregnant again, he'd whisk her off to some mountain hide-out, and not return her until the baby was half-way born.

He found himself wandering in the garden, and turned with his brooding to the inner section kept private for him and Alaine. He wandered aimlessly for a bit, then sat delicately on one of the benches by the pond in the scant shade of a jacaranda, which was just starting to colour with a scattering of purple against the blue of the sky. He listened to the bees, and the soft chirping of the honey eaters competing for the early nectar.

Then a squalling, and yelling, and a whirling about the edge of the water shattered his peace, and a body skidded along the path, and wrapped itself about his legs. He looked down into two imploring blue eyes, and up again into four sets of angry ones, as two serving girls, a nurse, and one of the multitude of midwifes, who had apparently taken over his household, descended upon him. His initial anger, directed at Wolverina, as the court had named the wild girl, was immediately redirected at the mid-wife.

"Enough!" he roared, allowing all his pent-up frustrations to govern his voice. The four halted as though they had run into a glass wall. Even the girl at his feet cringed. "What is the meaning of this racket?" he demanded in only a slightly lesser bellow.

It was unfortunate that the mid-wife took it upon herself to answer. The very sight of her enraged Fairein even more. Without allowing her to get more than the first word out, he sprang to his feet as well as he could spring with the girl's body still wrapped round his legs, and roared again, "Get you out of my sight!"

The mid-wife opened her mouth to speak again, but her instinct for self-preservation came to the fore, and she spun on her heel, sweeping her hesitant fellows along with her. Fairein watched the four stiff, highly offended backs disappearing from view, and suddenly laughed. A delighted giggle joined him from the ground, and Wolverina snapped straight like a green bow stick, and rose in a lithe arc to kneel before him. He looked down into her smiling eyes, and was suddenly struck by how beautiful she had become.

"What are you doing down there?" he asked laughing.

"Should I not kneel before my Prince?" she asked in return.

Fairein's eyebrows shot up in surprise. "Well!" he said, "You have certainly learned to speak, somewhat, since I've been away." He sat back down, and she sank back to sit on the path at his feet.

"I've learned a great deal," she told him with a pert grin, "but I haven't let that lot know." She glared in the direction the departing backs had disappeared.

He laughed again as he leaned forward like a father to ruffle her curls, and she lifted her head to meet his hand. He was suddenly surprised at how smooth, and silky her hair felt, and instead of ruffling it, he let his fingers slip through it. She moved almost imperceptibly against his legs, and he was surprised again by the feeling of sexual excitement that blossomed in his body, and the pleasurable stirring of his penis, as it swelled and stiffened beneath his clothes. She turned, and looked up at him, as though she understood the effect she had on him, and laid her arms across his thighs. He found it very difficult to continue to think of her as a child. Indeed as she moved, the front of her gown billowed out, and he could see down along the long curve of her throat to the sweet swelling of her breasts, and they were far from childlike. Suddenly, he had difficulty in breathing, and the swelling of his penis went from pleasure to pain.

When she dropped her chin on her arm, and rested her cheek lightly against his member, he had difficulty suppressing a groan. His hands trembled with the effort necessary to keep them from clutching her, and pressing her against him.

"You shouldn't sit there!" he managed to say through the tightness in his throat. His voice sounded forced, and strange, even to his ears.

She lifted her head slowly to look him in the eyes. "I'm sorry. I displease you?"

"No. No, of course not. It's just you'll get your gown dirty."

She laughed, sitting up straight, and twisting to face him. "Who cares? It's not much of a gown - look it's too big for me." She grasped the bodice, and pulled it out to illustrate her point, and she was right. It was too large, and it came away, and he saw the whole front of her body down to the tops of her legs. She wore no underclothes. She heard the sharp intake of his breath, and smiled up at him. Then she took his hand, turned the palm in, brought it to her lips, and kissed it, then rose on her knees, and tucked his hand in under the bodice and about her left breast.

The effect was galvanic. A great gasp burst from Fairein's lips, and he would have stood, but her clasp was strong. She rose, lithe and snakelike, and her body slid up along his until their lips met, and his body reacted despite him. His hands clasped her, and drew her even closer, and their kiss became more passionate, as her tongue darted in and out of his mouth.

When, at last, lack of breath forced them apart, he found that her gown was gone. She rose even higher, guiding his lips to her breast, and holding his head against her. Thought, and reason, were lost to him. Desire burned within him. She rose still higher, swinging a leg across his, and bringing his lips to the level of her navel where he smelt the exciting desire in her. Then she came down along his body, and he was surprised to discover that, at some time, she had opened his trousers, and his penis was standing free. She came down upon it. It met resistance there between her legs, and he realised, with a start, that she was virgin. He started to cry out in protest, and would have lifted her away, but she gripped him to her, and thrust herself down. Her hymen rent, and he burst into her with a great cry from both of them, hers of both triumph and pain; his of pure pleasure.

For a moment, when he looked into her eyes, he thought he saw something much older, and somehow snakelike, but her lips were seeking his again, and she was moving her lovely body against him, pressing him down, and back. All thought was submerged under the swirling tides of pleasure.

When reason returned, he found himself lying along the bench with the girl resting quietly on top of him. Conflicting emotions flickered in and out of his consciousness, but a glance at the sun sent them spinning from his mind. It was dinnertime. Someone would come looking for him. It could even be Alaine. With a croak, he lifted Wolverina off him, and staggered to his feet. "It's dinnertime. Quickly. We've got to get dressed."

He bent to pull up his trousers, and stopped in dismay. They were stained with bright, fresh blood. "My God!" he gasped.

Beside him, Wolverina rose, lifted the gown over her head, stepped calmly into the pond, and promptly sat down and bobbed about in the water.

"What in the Firetime are you doing?" he demanded.

"Come. Aren't you going to save me, or should I scream for help?"

"Damn it! We're wasting time!" he said, but he waded in obediently, and grabbed her as she blew bubbles.

But she laughed, and knelt in the water, and used her gown to sponge the blood off his trousers. "There." She smiled. "The stupid Wild Girl has delayed you, and got you wet, and now they'll have to hold dinner while you go and change." She laughed again, pleased with the expression on his face.

He was helping her from the water, and she was making convincing little noises of distress when Alaine's younger brother rounded the bend in the path calling for him. The youth stopped startled. "What happened?" he demanded.

"Oh. She just tripped up, and fell in. I thought she was going to drown," Fairein told him.

He stared at the bedraggled girl and grinned. "I'd have let her," he said, but there was no malice in his voice, only dry amusement.

Wolverina glared, and Fairein hastily bade the youth to hurry back, and explain that they were to start the meal without him, as he had to go and get changed.

They parted with barely a word at the entrance to Fairein's quarters. He wondered briefly where she was housed, and where she ate, but his mind was on getting into dry clothes as soon as possible.

The tale had obviously gone the rounds before he reached his place at the table. Alaine's young brother had the smug look of someone who had briefly held centre stage. Alaine was looking annoyed, but most others, who had experienced some of the antics of Wolverina first hand, were openly amused. He picked out her name, here and there, in the conversations that developed once more as he sat and began to eat. He was preoccupied and worried throughout the meal. Now that a good part of the rogue hormones had been drained from his body, he no longer felt the fierce desire for sex, or the ill will against those who had kept him from Alaine. He felt guilty, and remorseful, that he had been unfaithful. It was not uncommon in Elf society for a husband to take a mistress during his wife's pregnancy, especially amongst the nobility where most marriages were arranged affairs, but his had been a love match, and Alaine had a right to expect him to be faithful. He vowed not to let it happen again, and he decided that Wolverina would be removed from the palace, and housed in some other institution where her education could be better carried out. She could not be blamed for what had happened. After all, a wolf pack was not the place to learn the niceties of sexual, or moral, behaviour. Those things would have to be taught before she returned to the palace.

With that decided, his spirits rose, and after a couple of glasses of wine, he was once more smiling, even if his smiles for Alaine were a little strained.

He had no opportunity to put his plans for Wolverina into practice in the next couple of days, however. He was kept fully busy in planning sessions with Olvar, and his other generals, in visiting the camps where conscripted youth were being given preliminary training, and the workshops, and forges, where the trappings of war were being manufactured at top speed. There was nothing like the threat of a full-scale invasion by the Nasdarks to galvanise his people into action, but even here, there were very few who took the talk of an invasion from the south seriously.

When he did find a break in his schedule on the third day, and broached the subject with those who had been put in charge of Wolverine's welfare, two things had changed. His body had become charged with hormones again, and instead of distaste when he thought of the girl, pleasure and excitement were uppermost in his mind. Her slim, perfectly formed body began to haunt his idle moments, and the memory of their uninhibited love making was enough to send a thrill of pleasure coursing through his body. Alaine had welcomed his love making, and had certainly given, and received, pleasure, but hers had been an essentially passive role. He could not imagine her making love the way Wolverina had.

The second thing was the attitude of the girl's tutors. All professed instant dismay at the thought of sending her away. He was surprised. A few days before, he was certain they would have welcomed the suggestion with cries of gladness. Now he got a catalogue of how well she was doing at her lessons, and how well she was behaving. Her language tutor explained happily that she had learned her name, and had spoken five words almost perfectly. He fully expected to be able to start on sentence construction in a couple of weeks, and then he felt that she would be able to carry on a simple conversation. The nurse, who had been charged with seeing to her more practical needs, reported, equally happily, that she had accepted cooked meat for the first time, and actually seemed to prefer it to the raw meat she had insisted on previously. She had even learned to use the toilet he was told, delicately.

He came away from the discussion puzzled, undecided, and not a little amused. Wolverina had certainly made fools of her tutors. He remembered her telling him that she had learned a lot but had not let "them" know it. Her speech, however, had been almost perfect. How she had got it so without practice, he couldn't imagine. He decided to ask her when next he got her by herself. When she did decide to let them know how much they had taught her, they were in for a surprise, he thought.

He did see her next day. She greeted him with gladness, but in no way differently from any other time. They were not alone, and, as she had done before, she crept close to him, but said nothing, and stayed, unobtrusively, in the background. Her closeness was a source of excitement that alternated between producing pleasure and irritation. His penis seemed to be continuously erect and he had trouble keeping his mind on what he was doing. He recognised the conditions that had led to him losing control previously, and decided that, despite her tutors' protests, she would have to go. He would tell Olvar what had happened, and put the arrangements into his hands on the morrow.

It didn't happen. That night she came to his bed. He had been up with affairs of state until late. It was still warm when he retired despite the earliness of the season, and some over-solicitous servant had built the fire too high. The room was stifling. He had opened the windows, and pulled back the drapes. It let the moonlight in, but a cool breeze stirred about him, and that compensated for the light that threatened to keep him awake. He stripped off, and lay on top of the covers waiting for the room to cool.

There came a light tap on the door, and before he could rise or call, it opened, and she slipped through. At first, with a great gush of joy, he thought it was Alaine sneaking in to visit him, as she stood, all cloaked against the night, in the beam of moonlight from the first window. Then she stepped into the darkness between the windows, and reappeared in the next beam without the cloak. She shimmered in something white and flowing, that the breeze stirred about her, and he knew her to be not Alaine but Wolverina. Disappointment warred with excitement and desire. Then she was gone into the shadows again and came into the next beam without the gown, all naked and silvered by the moon.

She stood looking at him where he lay in the moonlight, and then she seemed to float towards him, in and out of the moonbeams, coming closer and closer, and more and more, beautiful, until she seemed to hover above him while he drank in her beauty like a draft of wine, before she dropped into his waiting arms.

Once more he was astonished, and delighted by her sexual appetite and energy. Her body demanded all he could give, and when he fell back exhausted, she slipped from him and ran to where she had dropped her cloak. She returned with a flask and glasses of wine, and he eagerly took the proffered glass and drank deeply. There was no scent, or taste, to warn him that something had been added to the wine, something distilled in hellish laboratories from the venom of snakes many kilometres to the south, and carried with great care all the dangerous distance to the girl. He only knew that, on putting down the empty glass, he found his energy miraculously restored, his penis engorged and erect again, and his body wild with lust. She came just as eagerly to him, and he was lost in a whirling paean of ecstasy.

How long it lasted, he had no way of knowing, but suddenly he was completely and utterly exhausted. He lay on his back so weary that it was an effort to breathe. She sat cradling his head in her lap, bending over him - rocking backward and forward. Her face was pooled in darkness but the moon shone on the dark nipples of her breasts as they moved backwards and forwards above his face. He watched them, fascinated by their black beauty in the silver mounds of glowing flesh. She was speaking softly, lovingly, as to an infant. His eyes focused on one nipple as it moved backwards and forwards. Her voice cocooned him, soft, hypnotic. He sank further and further under her spell, his brain too tired to tell him what was happening. He didn't know when her soft voice became hard and demanding. He didn't know that exhausted though he was, his body obeyed her every command. He didn't know what sexual pleasures he brought her or in what lurid, perverted ways he did so.

Then, when at last she was satisfied, she lay beside him, and her mind entered his, worming deep down into his unconscious being, and, like a worm turning an apple rotten, carefully began to alter his memories. Little things she changed, things that would go almost unnoticed, but things that gave her almost as much perverted pleasure as the hours of sex that had gone before.

In the morning, she was gone. Fairein woke late, and feeling as though he had been on an all-night drinking session. His head ached. His bones ached. In fact, his whole body ached, but most of all his testicles ached. He groaned, and sat up, holding his head. He thought of Wolverina, and groaned again, as, even in that state, his body began to pump his penis erect at the thought. This time there was no feeling of distaste, no guilt, only an eagerness to hold her again. Of Alaine he gave only a fleeting thought. She no longer seemed important to him.

He knew he should be up seeing to the new recruits, but even the coming war seemed unimportant. In fact, he wondered if the Nasdark might have made the whole thing up, and was even now, back home, telling all his nation what fools he had made of the Elves, and how he had got a guided tour right across the Elfin Kingdom, something no other Nasdark had ever managed to do.

At last, Olvar came to get him, and he reluctantly made the effort to get dressed and to take up his duties. He was scheduled to go on an inspection tour of the token guard that they kept on the Western Borders. No one really expected an attack from there, for there was where the secretive Drarks ruled their mountain fastnesses. The Drarks asked nothing from anyone except to be left alone. No one tried to pass through their lands without permission for, invariably, the uninvited who entered were never heard from again. Still there were those amongst the Elves who argued that the Red Queen might have managed to get agents even there, and insisted on the guard being strengthened. They had done so mostly with old men, and youths, who were considered unsuitable for real battle. The old men however, were mostly proud old veterans, unhappy at being shunted off to so isolated a region. It was essential that they be shown the same courtesies as the rest of the troops.

Thus, it was that in the afternoon, with his buttocks still sore from his earlier tours, and his bones aching from his sexual excesses, Fairein set off with little grace or good humour, to visit the West. He had not seen Wolverina all day, and he had barely paused to bid a grumpy farewell to Alaine, before he and Olvar, with a small contingent of guards, rode out on a trip that would take them the best part of a month to complete.

He hadn't seen Wolverina mainly because she, too, was paying a price for her sexual excesses. Her breasts, and genitals, were bruised, and sore, and she walked only with difficulty. Adriana, Fairein's Great Aunt, noted it when she passed her in the courtyard at-lunchtime.

"That one didn't sleep alone last night," she commented loudly with a malicious smile to her companion, the Lady Alicia.

"Oh. How so? Why do you say that?" Alicia had been much diverted by gossip concerning others since she had been made to suffer being the object of it after the unfortunate break-up of her betrothal to Descot.

"Just look at the way she walks. She looks as if she's holding a very large, and very hot potato, in her you-know-what."

Alicia laughed. "Hush. She'll hear you. But by the Firetime, you are right. She does walk so. But who would take her to his bed. Surely none of the young men about the Prince."

It was Adriana's turn to laugh. "You don't have to worry. The creature can hear well enough, but she can't understand more than a dozen words, so I am told. I doubt anyone with any breeding would have touched her. I don't think many would be too anxious to risk their manhood on a she-wolf. She's just as likely to bite it right off, if all they say about her is true. Do you know, she wouldn't eat anything but raw meat when they first brought her in? Should have left her with the wolves if you ask me. Besides, methinks, it'd have to be an overly energetic lad to make her walk so. No. She's probably been visiting the recruit camps. I wonder if Fairein knows. He seems to think the world of the little bitch. God knows why. He wouldn't be too pleased to hear of it, I'd warrant."

"Well. He'll not hear about it from me. Come on, or they'll have started lunch without us. Then Alaine will be glaring at us when we come in. She's getting very touchy lately. Methinks it would be better for all concerned if those interfering old crones of midwifes would mind their own business, and let those two get together. Oh! Do come on!"

She must have heard the conversation, but Wolverina walked on with lumpish indifference into the kitchen where she sat at her accustomed place as far from the fire as possible, and wolfishly ate the food proffered. There was little of the grace and beauty about her that had so captivated Fairein. If any came near while she was eating, her top lip curled upwards in a snarl, and she clutched protectively at the remaining food. Even the lowest servants turned away in disgust at the way she ate, but at least she now accepted cooked meat, and they didn't have to watch the blood streaming down her chin from raw meat, as they used to. She was treated with a certain grudging respect, however. This was both because she seemed to be a favourite of Fairein's, and because she could engender fear. Not long after she had been brought in, a couple of kitchen maids had decided that she should be forced to do the more unpopular tasks. They had recruited a couple of companions, and the four had set about the task of forcing her to scrub out the great cooking pots. The melee had lasted about three minutes before the guards managed to rescue the chastened four. The sisterhood had considerable work to patch up their wounds.

Fairein would have been surprised, indeed, to have seen her as his servants did. There was little chance of that, however. He had lunched with his men, and was already some miles from home. He rode a gentler mount than his usual war-horse, and had seen that his servants fitted him with a more padded saddle. Still, he wasn't comfortable, and he had three long days riding to reach the nearest keep where he could reasonably call a halt. To increase his annoyance the weather turned wet and cold, with a bitter wind from the south, and a fine drizzle slanting across their path.

The warriors endured silently as was their custom and their nature. To complain would have lessened them in the eyes of their fellows. Olvar rode as though wind and rain touched him not. He did not even hunch his shoulders or turn his face from the blast. He rode straight in the saddle, and expected his warriors to do likewise. Fairein came close to hating him that first day on the road.

Despite a worsening in the weather, Fairein actually grew more comfortable on the second day. His youth, and good health, allowed him to regain some measure of vigour quickly, and by the end of the third day, he was almost fully recovered, physically at least.

As darkness threatened to overtake them, they were challenged by the sentries on the outskirts of the camp that housed the first of a line of troops that kept the Western Borders. These were in possibly the safest areas of the Kingdom, being protected by almost unscaleable ramparts of the Western

Mountains on the one hand, and the entire width of the Elfin Kingdom on the other. The Mountains were further protected by the presence of the Drarks who had always been non-aggressive, if not actually friendly to the Elves, but, what was more important, also not friendly to the enemies of the Elves.

Fairein looked about with pleasure as he was escorted with much pomp into the camp. These were mostly old Warriors recalled from semi-retirement, and sent to guard what few considered needed guarding. Yet, there was no sign of slackness in their camp or bearing. He had come unannounced, and probably unexpected, but all was in excellent order, and men went about their evening tasks with precision and efficiency. He sighed as he recalled the lack of military precision in the South, and wondered if he should take Olvar's advice and demote all the southern commanders, and send some of these to replace them.

He slept in a comfortable bed that night, and next morning, clothed in a clean and dry outfit, and after a very pleasant and adequate breakfast, and with the sun shining at last, he and his party rode out of camp actually looking forward to the day's toil. Although he would not have welcomed a prolonged hard gallop, Fairein's buttocks were much improved, and he rode with only slight discomfort. Only a minor disquiet, as they set out that morning, was a feeling of guilt that in his warm bed he had dreamed of Wolverina, and not of Alaine, and he could not really bring himself to regret it. Even when he made a conscious effort to recall Alaine's beauty, and the nights of love they had enjoyed, he felt no arousal, however, the mere thought of Wolverina sent his blood coursing.

Just after a picnic lunch beside the fast flowing Wheyle stream, the group turned aside to visit the old Dardane Valley and Castle. Dardane had once been a stronghold occupied by Fairein's distant ancestors when the Elf nation was young. The valley itself formed a kind of stronghold. A high range bulged out from the western mountains, forming almost a semicircle about a flat plain, covering some five hundred hectares. High terraces on the sides of the mountains showed that the basin had once been almost filled with water, and must have been a large, deep lake in the mountains. At some time, however, the water found a fault in the outer wall, or an earthquake had opened a narrow cleft, and the lake had poured out to form the Dardane, which now wandered in loops across the plain, and chattered over a series of small rapids as it came through the cleft, which, at its narrowest, was but five arm spans wide.

Through this narrow pass, a path, barely wide enough to take a laden packhorse, had been cut, and, in some places, tunnelled. In times past, when the Elves had been less powerful and sure of themselves, Dardane had formed a well garrisoned and provisioned stronghold, kept ever ready to form a last refuge. More than once, an invading army had foundered against the walls about the entrance to the cleft, dubbed the Wolf's Throat by the Elves. Then it had been important indeed in elfin society. Kings kept seats there, and all the noble families lived, for part of the year at least, within its forbidding walls. However, now, after generations of secure borders, during which the Elves had felt little need for such a refuge, the old dwellings had been allowed to fall into decay. The city lay in ruins. Only a few farmers tended scattered fields along the banks of the stream, and all else had returned to woodland.

Still, almost in the centre of the plain, stood that which Fairein had come to inspect. It was the old citadel built on the last hump of a spur that ran down from the mountains almost into the middle of the plain. Grim it looked, and forbidding, with its great stone walls, dark with moss and hung with lichens. It had stood high, and strong, even before the ancient warriors had worked mightily to cut away the base of the cliffs on which it stood, so that the walls of rock were smooth, and either vertical, or even slightly overhanging, making them almost impossible to scale. The only approach wound up the side of the mountain, and crept along a thin saddle to the great gate that faced the West. Vast labours had cut the sides of this path so that it formed a narrow road bordered by cliffs that dropped some sixty to eighty feet on either side. Overlooking this approach were two mighty towers tiered with balconies, from which a thousand kneeling archers could rain arrows down upon a foe. Great rounded stones were kept in readiness from where they could be rolled down along the path, crushing any that stood upon it, should a roof of shields frustrate the archers. Reservoirs of pitch had been kept filled in the old days, so that fiery bombs could the catapulted all along the road.

This fortress had never quite been allowed to fall into ruin, and Fairein, gazing up at it from the valley floor, smiled grimly. It was as he remembered it. There he would bring the women and children, if the need arose, and there the Elves would make a last stand. Once more it would be garrisoned and provisioned, the water tanks would be filled, and the ancient underground pipes would be cleaned so that water would make its secret way into the wells.

***

They spent the rest of the day visiting the local farmers, and recruiting what labour there was available to start preliminary repairs to the roads and bridges. These would support the mass of men and materials that would be sent as soon as the party returned to the Palace.

For five more days, Fairien, with half his troops, rode northward along the base of the Western Mountains, visiting the tiny garrison towns and forts, while Olvar, with the rest of the men, rode to the south. To the North, the mountains rose higher and higher, until they climaxed in the great snow-covered knot, known simply as The Crags Of Thane. From that, the great range of Thrul swept along the Northern borders, forming a bulwark against the ravening Nasdarks. Long had those mountains served the Elves. The few passes were guarded by Elf and Nasdark alike. For generations, each had built fortifications higher and deeper, facing each other over a few hundred metres of no-man's-land. The passes were no longer passes, but in some cases would be more difficult to traverse than the surrounding peaks, even if some miracle brought peace and friendship to the two races.

Only in the Far East could the Elves venture northward if such was their wish, for the land of the Nasdarks was halted by the tiny Kingdom of Malravia, which had long allied to the white races of Donwin. Long had the Nasdarks craved for that land, but never had they felt strong enough to challenge the might of Donwin unaided. The last war between the Donwins and the black nations had seemed like an answer to their dreams, but it had ended in total failure. Few of the elite Troop they had sent had returned, and they had earned the lasting enmity of King Ungar, and were forced now to strengthen the guard on their northern borders, where once they could leave but token forces.

Fairein's party turned homeward once they had reached the northern borders. Those garrisons had been the first to be visited, and alerted, after the warning had come. They had been found already very conscious of the need to be watchful for spies, and lookouts had reported unusually high levels of activity by the Nasdarks all along the borders, though none had attacked the posts.

So it was that a little more than three weeks after leaving, Fairein came once more into sight of his palace, and was greeted by the usual blast of trumpets as his small contingent was seen by the sentries on the outer walls of the city.

Alaine was there to meet him according to custom, though now her pregnancy was clearly showing. He greeted her gladly, swinging from the saddle to take her in his arms and kiss her. For a few moments, all the old love swelled through him, but the Midwives soon fussed their way between them, and he found himself scanning the crowd, eagerly seeking the slim form of Wolverina.

She was nowhere about, but she came to his bed in the early hours of the morning, and there was no need of the poisoned wine to impel him to drive himself to exhaustion in her arms. Once more she commanded him in the secret hours.

As before, she followed him unobtrusively wherever she could, and soon, everyone was too occupied to worry about her, as Fairein put into operation his plans to get the Dardane back into use. As most of the young men had been recruited into the army and were busy training, there were few available to build. Stone masons and master builders were drafted, and older men eagerly came forward to add their effort. Fairein needed more, and strong young women were called for.

There was little difficulty mobilising large numbers of these, and within a fortnight of his return, Fairein could lead off the first contingent. Wolverina rode on one of the front wagons. Fairein, as he rode at the head of the long line, would have been surprised to have learned that he had ordered that she should be so placed. When she came to his tent at night, he accepted it without wonder that she could slip through his guards, though he did not know that he had given the orders that allowed it. Each night they made love until he was exhausted, and then he surrendered to her voice. She drove him to perverted acts of sex until she was at last satisfied, then she wormed into his mind.

It took another two weeks to organise the workers into task forces and to ensure that all leaders knew exactly what was required of them. Fairein worked long hours despite his obvious weariness, and Wolverina was never far from his side. She worked tirelessly, seeming ever wishing to please, and the work she did helped to dampen the resentment people felt at her relationship with Fairein. She was never allocated to any particular group, however, so, when Fairein was satisfied that all was in hand and left, her disappearance was hardly marked in the general effort. Any who wondered, assumed that the Prince had taken her along with him. No one noticed her slip away to join the mountain wolves.

Three of these, she was forced to kill, before she became undisputed leader of the pack. Then she led them on a series of raids on the herds being brought into the valley, but she was careful to strike in widely spaced areas, and selected the less valuable stock. Her pack fed well, and did not engender a great deal of anxiety.

Then she turned her attention to the mountains, and the wolves led her by their secret ways through the wilderness to the land of the Nasdarks, where she was eagerly awaited.

Chapter 4

Summons

"There is something there. I'm sure of it, Giant." Dana pulled her mount to a halt, and stared out across the plain to the east. The Giant shrugged, and allowed his stallion to ease to a halt beside her. The Drark, from his position in the fore, swung to face them.

"There is much out there," he said mildly, gazing out over the patterned landscape of hill and vale, farm and forest, and the far glitter of sand where the desert began. "What thing irks you, Lady? You have been troubled near this time these last five days at least."

"I know, Drark. I have not said anything as I know not what it is, but something has whispered about my mind these last evenings."

"The Red Queen?" queried the Giant, his brow creasing in a frown, and his hand instinctively creeping towards his sword. "Think you she spies us out? If it is true she knows what happened to the other weapon, she'll expect us to come after this one."

"It could be so. I cannot say. Yet it seems not threatening. But more like the voice of one in need. It is as though one is calling for succour, but is too far away for me to hear."

"I would not put too much value on such feelings," declared the Giant. "Yon Queen is well versed in treachery, me thinks. I feel it best if we avoid contact as much as possible. I would not walk into ambush by enemies who hold the weapon."

Dana laughed grimly. "I doubt we'd even know of it." She looked at the high, snow-shrouded peaks that rose so close in the west, and shivered. Then she looked pointedly down at the almost imperceptible track they had been following. "This track will not last. Nothing has passed this way in months, especially not a dray, and I've seen no print of horses. What say you, Drark? Will we find our way into the mountains on this poor excuse for a path? And even if we do, do you think we have a hope of finding the weapon party on it?"

The Drark shrugged. "I fear I've come to doubt both, Lady. But somewhere a path must lead into them. This wall cannot go on forever."

"Try telling it that. We've come a long way this week, and there is no sign of a break. If this is the Red Queen hunting us, then she probably knows full well where we are, and what we are trying to do. Would it not be better to try to ambush her?"

"How so, Lady?"

"Tomorrow we could stop at this time. It is, after all, the time most honest travellers stop for the evening meal, and Giant and I could bond. Then, when she comes snooping around, could we not try to capture her mind? If we could surprise her, we might hold her for an instant, and get some useful thoughts before she broke away."

The Giant smiled wryly. "The idea is good, if dangerous. What if we couldn't control her, and she held us? She was far stronger than I when we faced her Demons."

"She had her Demons to channel her power then. She has no one here. Her cast must need be wide. If we were quick she wouldn't have time to focus. A quick grab at her thoughts and out again, and we lie low. I doubt she would gain much except a worry that might stop her spying for a while. If we're lucky, she could be seeking the other weapon rather than us, and then we'd know she knew not where it was, and could possibly get a hint to where it most likely is. Besides, what would she gain by trying to hold us? She couldn't do it for long enough to get her people here to attack us, and surely, she cannot twist our minds when we are aware. You were very tired, and unsuspecting, when she did it before, Giant."

The Giant grunted noncommittally, and urged his mount reluctantly forward. "It bears considering. I do not like it. Probably because I have felt that mind before, and would prefer not to again, but if this infernal blank goes on much more, we'll have to try something. If they have gotten into the mountains by a pass we missed, then, even if we do get in, we'll have no way of finding them."

Dana shrugged. "You are right. I sometimes think we are on a fool's mission, and the Queen already has the weapon, and is doing untold harm with it."

"Peace, Lady." murmured the Drark. "We can only do our best. This endless riding tears our nerves to no avail. Me thinks we should try this mind ambush even if to merely give us aim."

"Then so be it," said the Giant. "Now let us look for somewhere to camp. Our horses grow weary, and we may yet need their strength."

Night found the three camped beside a small stream that fell off the mountains and wandered through the foothills they had been traversing. The need to find a pass prevented them from following the edge of the plain where the riding was much easier. The few shepherds and hunters they met were wary of so unusual a company, and all declared the mountains impassable until much later in the season. All seemed to know of high passes that could be travelled in the height of summer, but none could imagine why such a party would want to use them. Only desperate hunters, and foolhardy shepherds, went there, they were told. The Firetime wolves, and worse, ravaged unbridled there, and few that entered, returned. All shook their heads when asked concerning another party either with a dray or all on horseback. They rode on discouraged.

Dana and the Giant bonded before sleeping, but they held contact for only a short time. Both were very tired and worried, and in dire need of sleep. It was the Giant's turn for first watch so they did little but confirm their love, and broke the contact. Dana fell asleep almost at once. The Drark smoked his evening pipe, gazing at the mountains and the faint stars above the glittering snows. The Giant sat with his back to a rock, and watched mainly the path they had travelled. An enemy would most likely come from that direction.

"Think you it would be better to forget this chasing after weapons, and go to the Vipands and seek news of the Red Queen there? Where she is, the weapon will come."

The Drark stirred out of some reverie of his own. "Do you think we could get help from Melina's father? It would only make more sense if we had someone in mind to seek word from. To blunder into that den of snakes would be very dangerous now. I do not think the priests of Sturk are likely to be noted for their forgiving natures."

The Giant chuckled grimly. "You speak more than the simple truth. If we were to ride roughly south-east, we should be able to reach Tander in about three weeks - if we buy fresh horses every four or five days. We could get a message from Melina for her father. From what she says, he is likely to help us. Another three weeks to get us back here, and six to eight more at least to get through the desert and the Femins. That's well into summer. The weapon would be in the hands of the Red Queen for sure. On the other hand, if we ride hard for the Vipands now, we'll save six weeks. By keeping close to the mountains like this, we'll have cover. We might be able to find hunters or outlaws, who are not in love with the snakes. Hunters are independent folk in my experience, and outlaws are seldom religious. They might be prevailed upon to tell us where this Queen has her realm."

"If they know. It is strange that Melina lived in the Western Marches, and knew little of the Red Queen. Have you thought that she could be in, or over, the mountains here?"

"She seemed most known by the Vipands, and least known in Fenderland."

"True. But had Ungar died outside Mandanna, instead of Mondar, think you that the Red Queen would not now be well known in far Donwin? Yet, anyone seeking her realm on the edges of Donwin would find it not. This power of the mind seems to travel far and fast."

"You mean she could be anywhere, and we wasting our time?"

"Not altogether. The Vipands have another claim to be close to her. They appear to be the first to come under her dominion, and that, not fully yet. Sturk is still very strong. Or, is it possible, that the priests of Sturk do her bidding and do not know? Me thinks a priest might not know that the commands that come into his mind are those of a Red Queen, and not of a Snake God. Especially when both are tainted with evil."

The Giant cursed softly. "You make our task seem impossible. Can you see any hope?"

"We must always hope, else Death is welcome. I think Dana's plan to capture this spying mind is worth trying. It may be one of the Queen's servants, even one of those we seek, who keeps track of us. If we captured one such as that, we might learn much. By all accounts your powers are very strong Giant. If you could hold a servant in thrall, you might learn where both the Queen and the weapon lie, and much more."

"You are right. You have thought well on this. I do not much like the idea of capturing minds, but I am happy to have a plan - anything rather than aimless seeking."

The following afternoon found the three on top of a high hill bordering the still impenetrable wall of mountains. The view was breathtaking for any who had mind to look. The snow-capped mountains rose almost two thousand metres in a great unbroken wall. Streams of melt water tumbled down giant cliffs, or hung as misty curtains that blew backwards and forwards with the errant winds. Giant eagles rode the thermals along the tops of the cliffs, and, at times, swept out over the foothills in great curves. To the east, the farms and forests were giving way to grasslands with scattered patches of thornbush. The Firetime Sands were now visible as a silver smudge on the northern horizon. The lands of the Small Ones could be seen as a verdant swathe between the grass lands and the farms of Fenderland.

The three were not enjoying the scenery, however. They were much more inward looking. Dana and the Giant sat hand-in-hand, hovering on the verges of bond, so each was aware of the other's mind, but could also act independently. The Drark sat on a high rock and surveyed the land about. The horses grazed quietly nearby, but had not been unsaddled for the night. The spot had been picked carefully, and well-scouted. They held a commanding position, but a long, smooth spur led down to a wide expanse of forest and broken hills, should a fast escape be required. It would take many men to trap them.

Now they sat tensely as the hour of the visitation approached. Dana felt it first. She squeezed the giant's hand, and sucked power from his mind until her head felt near to bursting, and threw her awareness out like a striking viper along the tenuous link. There was a snap across space, and a moment of fright and confusion, and then she had a mind, many minds, struggling in fear, flicking in and out of bond. Dana gasped and rapidly lowered the surge of power, for the minds she gripped belonged to the Sisterhood. She was in contact with the Elves.

She broke connection, bonded with the Giant for the instant it took for him to become aware of the situation, and then reached back to the

Sisterhood with a much gentler probe. She held bond for only a short time, then broke it and bonded once more with the Giant. Then they turned to the Drark who was watching with something almost like excitement in his eyes.

"It was the Sisterhood seeking us, Drark. Alaine is worried, and wants us home. They have been warned that the Red Queen is seeking to destroy all Elf women and war is imminent, both from the Nasdarks and from the south, which could only be the Vipands, unless she has the weapon and is committing her own people."

"Why does she wish to destroy Elf women? What has she against your kind, Lady?"

"Because, together, we were too powerful for her and her Red Demons. She knows she cannot gain complete power while Elf women can challenge her. So she has brought war with the aim to destroy the Elf nation and every Elf female. What is also worrying Alaine is that Fairein is acting strangely."

"How strangely?"

"The Sisterhood does not know. Alaine would not tell them exactly what is wrong. It would seem like being disloyal to her husband, I suppose, and, after all, it was a love match. She would not like to say anything against him. But it seems all know that he has been giving some strange orders about the deployment of troops, and then countermanding them, and sometimes not even appearing to remember what orders he has given. People are saying that the responsibility, so soon after his wounding, has affected his mind. Our forces are confused when they desperately require clear leadership."

"So, what do we do now, Lady?" Both turned to the Giant.

He shrugged. "I think we now know where the weapon is headed. It is imperative that we get there first. The Elves do well enough against the Nasdarks, but the Vipands' poison, and the Firetime weapon - they know nothing of fighting those. If only we could bond with strike leaders."

"At least with the Snakes marching, it will be easier to cross their lands. We may be able to interest some Femins in the war if it is mainly against women."

They broke camp next day with much greater cheer than they had for many days. A definite goal ahead, and relief from having to ride the interminable foothills in case they missed some pass, raised their spirits. They moved down to the edges of the plain, and rode swiftly, angling north-easterly to cut the edge of the desert somewhere near the place they had exited over twelve months before.

At times they glimpsed Small Ones leaving their herds, and disappearing into the distance, but they had no time to spare to make contact as they would have liked to. It would have been better if they could have replenished their food supplies before entering the desert. They discussed slaughtering one of the abandoned cattle but thought better of it.

With the knowledge of where to locate oases, they could travel quicker, and only a couple of weeks brought them to the village of the water poisoners. They approached cautiously but were greeted warmly enough. They found the village in a state of uneasy peace. The women who had remained had tried to revert to the Femin's way of life. The men had resisted. Neither could live without the other, so they had broken into two armed camps that co-operated only as necessary. When the travellers returned as proof that the Firetime Sands could be crossed, some of the men prepared to head south to start a new life in Fenderland.

The three stayed only long enough to rest the horses, and pushed on to the land of the Femins. Here, their stay was more prolonged. The First One was interested in their travels, but more interested in their knowledge of the Red Queen.

They had been well into the land of the Femins before they were discovered, and brought before the First One. She eyed them balefully for a few moments as they approached. Dana gave the closed fist salute of the Femin warriors. "Greeting, First One. We have returned."

"That I see, Child. So the Firetime Sands can indeed be crossed. Is there danger for my people from the South?"

"Not from the South, First One, though there is a large Kingdom called Fenderland there. Most people there believe that the Sands cannot be crossed, also. But, even if they thought otherwise, they do not appear warlike, and, under the present government at least, I see no danger of attack from there."

"I see. That is fair news, but we will patrol more vigilantly in that quarter just the same. Now. What news of your quest? Did you find your Island of Legend, and do you return with the thing you sought?"

"We found the Island, First One, and we found the thing we sought, but we have taken it to Donwin, fought in the war there, returned to the Island, recovered one Firetime weapon, and went seeking another since then."

The First One frowned darkly. "That is a long catalogue of deeds for so short a time, Child, and would be more believable if it didn't mean you must have passed twice through this land without my knowledge."

Dana smiled and shook her head. "No, First One, we found many strange things in the island. The Before Time seems much closer there. We travelled North, and South again, by ship on the oceans to the east. It used the wind to make it move. It was very quick."

"I see. There is much I would know of the outside world, but first I would hear of this Red Queen you seek. She has cost me six of my best warriors, and you six of your offspring, Giant."

The Giant started. "How so, First One?"

"Six of the warriors who attended you became pregnant, and four to you, Drark. They were excused duties early in their pregnancies as the midwifes were concerned that the babies fathered by you, Giant, might grow large in them and cause them distress. We sent them to the valley of rest. They were betrayed. The Snakes were let in, and tried to carry them off, but they were true warriors, and chose to fight, weaponless though they were. The Snakes slew them all. They managed to rouse the guard, however, and those Snakes paid dearly." She glowered around at the assembled warriors, anger bright in her eyes. "We were betrayed for the first time in our history, and we would dearly like to know the traitor."

The Giant sighed. "You have an agent of the Queen amongst you," he said. Then he went on to describe the red-headed warrior, and her actions, and the poison she had whispered into his mind as he slept, and how Dana, and he, had found the false memories when they bonded.

The First One listened intently. At the mention of the red-haired warrior, a murmur had swept the hall, but the First One gestured to the Giant to continue. He was not interrupted until he stopped speaking, and then a flood of questions kept he and Dana busy until the company were called to the afternoon meal.

As they walked to the large mess hall where the First One ate with her warriors, the significance of the red-haired warrior was explained. She had disappeared on the fatal night, and it was believed that she had been captured, and taken by the small contingent of Snakes that had made good their escape. She had been believed a coward only. In answer to the Giant's question, the First One shook her head. She hadn't been pregnant. In fact, she should not have coupled with the Giant at all, since she had been but two days out of menstruation leave, and was most unlikely to conceive, but she had twice taken the place of warriors reluctant to fulfil that duty. Those two had been doing double duty in the most dangerous spots on the border ever since their crime had been discovered, and probably owed their lives to the lack of activity along the border since the raid, which was most likely caused by the Snakes' preoccupation with preparations for the attack on the Elves.

The Giant was relieved to find that he was not required to impregnate warriors on this occasion. In fact, a considerable change had taken place in the Femin's attitude towards him and the Drark. Dana was still treated as the leader of the party, but the Giant and Drark were given warrior status. They were the first males ever to be invited to eat with the warriors, and no restrictions were put on their movements. Apparently the Femins maintained some contact with the wild tribes in the mountain country to the east of their lands, and the story of the King's Hundred, and the downfall of the Red Queen's Demons, had reached even there. The tales had been highly exaggerated, and, as they had good cause to believe the three travellers were still in the South, they had not connected them with the ones who had apparently descended from the skies on steeds of fire, turned the tide of war, accomplished unbelievable feats of healing, and then vanished once more into the heavens. Dana's description of the battle, though far less dramatic than that of the tribesmen, had the ring of truth, unmistakable to these women who lived in almost constant warfare. Heroic deeds on the battlefield were the one thing that could win their respect, and so the Giant and Drark enjoyed what, in a less dour society, would have been almost hero worship.

Late into the night, continuing discussion inevitably brought up the subject of the Firetime weapons. Dana had to describe in great detail the effects of the weapon's blast.

It was very late when Dana formally asked for aid in the coming conflict. The First One stared at her grimly for some minutes. "We have never fought outside our boundaries except in raids against those who first harmed us. Why should we change our ways now? I have sympathy for the Elves, but my duty is to my people. If we fought your wars we must lose many warriors - who then will keep the Snakes from our doors?"

The Giant answered before Dana could speak. "The Red Queen, My Lady, is vastly ambitious. She would rule the world. The Snakes are her people and your deadly enemies. If they carry their poison, and the Firetime weapon against the Elves, then the Elves, unaided, and attacked on two sides, will surely be destroyed. Do you doubt that, sooner or later, you will face the victorious Snakes, augmented with warriors from captured nations corrupted by the Vipand religion, and armed with a weapon that will blast your warriors from their horses long before they can reach bowshot? Who, then, will keep the Snakes from your doors?"

The First One sat very quietly. A murmur of anger or disbelief ran through the assembled warriors. Then all became still, waiting for their leader to speak. "I'll think on what you say, Giant. I cannot commit my warriors on your word alone. I will send people out to find the truth of things, and then this assembly will decide. For now, rest. Tomorrow you shall have fresh horses and escort to the North-west border area where you might cross into the lands of this Lord Moska - though I would not trust any Snake. Still, if they march on the Elves, they would have to travel through the Western or Eastern mountains to avoid the Kersh and the Tandors. It would do them no good to try to fight their way through, unless that weapon is even worse than you say, Giant. Could it so easily get them through?"

The Giant nodded. "An army, unwarned of its danger, who rode out to meet the Snakes on open plain, in battle array, would be utterly destroyed in the first couple of minutes. Those warned, who stayed in hills, and under cover, might live longer, but could not stop their foes, who would only have to march on open ground. No doubt the first city they came to would be taken, and the people held hostage. After a while the mere knowledge of the weapon would bring nations to their knees. However, we do not know if the Queen yet has the weapon, or if she will give it over to the Snakes. We once thought she might keep one to guard her home rather than risk the chance that somehow it might fall into our hands and be used against her."

"That is a question I would have you answer. When you won the first weapon, why did you not keep it to use against your enemies? Now you would have had less to fear from Snakes or anyone else."

"No, First One, you are wrong. If I had such a weapon, I would have no friends. What ruler would not kill to possess it in these troubled times? Would you not seek to take it from me to keep your borders against the Snakes? Would not the Kersh? Would not the Elves themselves? It is the Firetime that we have to fear. Would you have me return that to the land?"

"You would indeed have to guard such a weapon well. But did you not wish to make yourself King? If all you say is true, you could have done so. Could you not?"

"Not a king, but a tyrant, Lady. A tyrant who lived in fear of everyone about him. Who could trust no one. Who would have to instil fear even in his own children to survive. I would not want that sort of life."

"Perhaps you speak truth, but I would not be so squeamish. I would dearly love to hold such a weapon when next the Snakes come raiding."

"Only, me thinks, if they do not hold one also."

"What! There are more?"

"There is the one we returned to Tasmanka. How many others are there, I do not know."

"Could they be stolen?"

"Not so easily now...but, yes. If a country wanted them dearly enough - then surely they could do at least as well as the Red Queen."

"Then the Firetime would indeed be returned."

"That is so."

The Giant's last words seemed to fall into a pool of silence. All in the assembly seemed to be staring into the embers of the fire contemplating an uncertain, and dangerous, future. The First One sighed. "I would the world would let us be. We want only to live our own lives in our own land. That is not too much to ask, surely, with a world so wide?"

"It is just that Right that we fight for, First One," Dana said sadly.

"Eyah! You've done your share of fighting, Elf warrior, all honour to you. But go you and rest this night, and go you on your way tomorrow. If things are as bad as you say, then maybe it is time for the Femins to ride to battle, and show that we, who but carry swords, are a force for Red Queens to fear as well as Elf Ladies."

Two nights later, the three with their escort of Femins, killed a Vipand border post, and crossed once more into the lands of the Snakes. When it was certain no alarm had been raised, the Femins turned back, and Giant, Dana, and Drark cantered grimly through the night, intending to ride only at night, and to hide during the day. They were travelling close to the Western Mountains so that they could use the rough country to hide in during the day, and because, if they did encounter Vipands, it would probably be Lord Mosca's people.

They encountered a shepherd herding a small flock of sheep in the foothills. He was young for his trade, and obviously took them for monsters down out of the mountain. They came upon him suddenly in the early morning. Unfortunately for him, he had started his flock moving in the early dawn, before the three had gone into hiding, and his dog had set up a fierce barking so that he saw them at once while he was still half asleep. It seemed to him that he had fallen into a nightmare. He had never seen a Giant before, much less a Drark, and he didn't take time to inspect Dana. He tried to run, but the horses bore down on him in a few seconds. He turned in a desperate effort to fight with only his shepherd's crook, but the Giant's horse hit him before he had it fully raised. He crumbled to the ground with his hands above his head, fully expecting to die. The Giant swung down, picked him up by the scruff of the neck, and made a swift check to see that he harboured no snakes, then set him down, none too gently, on his feet. His sheep scattered, while the dog jumped about in a snarling, barking, frenzy, as it tried to decide whether it should attend to the sheep or protect its master. It ended up by doing neither until the Drark leant down from his horse, smacked it on the rump with the flat of his sword, and while it was still yelping, sent it with a few short words after the sheep. The shepherd looked even more dejected when he lost even that small support.

"Where is Lord Moska?" growled the Giant, "I would speak with him."

The quaking youth looked up in evident surprise. It dawned on him slowly that the monsters could speak, and were not intent on killing him at once. The longer they talked the longer he had to live. "He...he's not here," he offered looking around wildly. "He's gone to war. In...in the North." He tried to think of something more to say to keep them occupied, but his mind went blank. "Lord!" he managed through his chattering teeth.

"When?" demanded the Giant.

"When? When? ...Last week. No, not last week. The week before. Yes, Lord. The week before. After Sturk's Day. He went to war. That way." He pointed vaguely towards the North-east.

"How many men guard the house?"

"None, Lord. I mean many, Lord. Old men and young, but very strong - good fighters. You would not want to attack there. Sturk said all must go - even shepherds, with only sticks to fight with." His eyes focused on Dana for the first time. "You're a girl!" he gasped.

"Not quite," she told him. "Just answer the questions, and you won't be hurt."

"Who do they go to fight?"

"I don't know, Lord. Some said the Kersh. Others say the Femins. My fath...master...said they are going to the North, past the Kersh, to fight Elves. I do not know."

"You are a strong looking young fellow, old enough to fight. Why are you not with them?" It was the Drark who asked out of the sudden silence.

The youth looked stricken. "I...I was sent with the sheep."

"Not a lot of sheep," observed the Drark. "You speak rather well for a shepherd, and have cleaner fingernails and teeth than most I've known. You know, Giant, he doesn't even smell like a shepherd. I would say he bathed within the last two days, which is strange, considering how cold the water is. Under all that dirt and rags, he looks a lot like a certain lady we know."

"You mean Melina?" Dana asked, staring intently at the youth who had started ever so slightly at the name. "Her younger brother, Danch, perhaps?"

At this the youth visibly gasped. "You knew my sister?" He looked at them again. "It was you. You were there when she died. You were the captives. My father told me...a giant, and a lady, and a...a"

"Drark." said the Drark.

"Drark. I've never heard of a Drark before. You escaped when the High Priest was carried up to Sturk on a column of Fire--or so the priests said-- but my father said he saw no column of fire. My father said that there were four of you who escaped, but the priests said the fourth was a Femin who helped you."

"The fourth was your sister, Danch. She is alive and well, and lives in a country to the south. She is married and will be a mother by now." Dana smiled.

"The High Priest was not carried up to Sturk was he? What happened?"

"The High Priest was going to kill your sister after molesting her. It seems she insulted him by not wishing to become a handmaiden. The Giant awoke from the sleeping poison and killed the High Priest--on a statue of Sturk, Melina said--so perhaps you could say he did go to Sturk that night even if it was not on a column of fire. Melina asked to come with us. Drark and I were still asleep. She helped get us away. But you haven't answered our question yet. Why are you here?"

"My mother made us do it. She thinks my father will be killed in the war; if not by the enemy, then by the priests. Another has gone in my place. I am looking for a place in the mountains. If my father does not come home, we'll have to live as outlaws, or we'll become slaves of the temple, or be sacrificed to Sturk."

"Do not try to live in the mountains. Make ready those you would take with you, and, when the time comes, take this token to the Femins, and ask for safe passage through their lands. It was given me by the First One herself, and she will honour it. Travel across the Firetime Sands until you come to Fenderland, and then seek the city Tander. There you will find your sister, now wife of Randeeshon, son of Glendeeshon, the Merchant, who will welcome you. There you will be able to live free of the priests of Sturk."

The youth took the token, and turned it over and over in his hand. "Your words are fair indeed, Lady, but how can I trust the lives of my mother and sister on them and this small thing. Why should you care what happens to us?"

It was the Giant who answered. "We do not know your mother or sister, and little of you to make your problems our concern, but Melina rode with us for many weeks and we grew to love her. Therefore, we would help those she loves. I cannot vouch for the Femins, but I believe that token would be honoured. I believe them trustworthy, but I would not take many men in your party. They might kill you before you could show the token. Send your sister with it. They are less likely to slay a woman - though they hold your women folk in scorn."

Danch seemed suddenly to come to a decision. "I'll take this to my mother and take council with her. She will be pleased to hear that Melina lives. Is there anything I can do for you in return for your kindness?"

"You could sell us one of your sheep. We have little meat left and no time to hunt. We are in need of speed. Do you know of a quick way across this country that we could ride without being seen?"

"The land has been almost emptied of men. Only the South is guarded against the Femins, and that by old men. If they find out, they'll raid and take the whole country. My father could not believe they were taking everyone. You could probably ride Sturk's road through the middle of his city with only the temple handmaidens to stay you. But you are going north to the war also, and you'll be fighting against my father. If you meet up with him - try not to kill him, please. He has no heart for this war or for the poison of snakes, but he had to obey the priests or we all would have died. I have dried meat in plenty, and time to hunt more if I need it. Take as much as you want, and good speed to you."

"Are there many more who think like your father?"

"I don't know. My father used to have many friends. They all seem to have died. No one comes to visit us now."

Danch's words proved to be accurate. The three decided to ride openly across the country at all speed. Only women, and the very old or young, were about, and they ran off in various states of disarray as soon as they saw the travellers. At one holding, they even came upon unguarded horses, and were able to choose fresh mounts. They encountered no opposition, but they were still very relieved when they rode into the Southern Vale of the Kersh and were greeted with all honour.

Here they heard more news of the Vipands. A large army had passed through the wastelands to the East of the vale. It was hill country, and largely forested. The Kersh had harried the force, at first, believing that an attack on the Vale was the army's objective, but they desisted when it was evident that no attack was aimed at them. They warned the Bartonians, and contented themselves with scouting the force. Because of the rough nature of the land, they could give no accurate estimate of the strength of the Vipands.

Much the same story greeted them when they reached Barton City. Again, they were greeted warmly by the people. Cant Barton was especially anxious to hear news of the force of Vipands that had passed through his country. He had lost more soldiers than the Kersh, as he had attempted to forbid the passage through his lands. Poison arrows had taken a terrible toll of his troops, and they had been driven from the field. However, to everyone's astonishment, the Vipands had not pressed home their advantage, but had continued on into the north.

After telling what they knew of the Red Queen, and of the Vipands' goal of wiping out the Elf women, the Giant pointed out that the Bartonians would not be so fortunate when the Vipands returned if they were victorious against the Elves. He suggested that they send a force to aid the Elves.

Cant, smarting from the defeat of his forces, could see the logic of his argument but was reluctant to deplete his forces even more. He was more inclined to provision his main cities and prepare for a siege. He did promise, however, to consult with his advisors and send what help they could afford. With that the three had to be content as they were in too much of a hurry to stay and argue.

Dana made contact with the Elves every afternoon, and the news was not encouraging. The Nasdarks were attacking all along the border, and Fairein was drawing more and more of his forces away from the south, and sending them to the north. The Sisterhood warned him again and again of the approach of the Vipands, but he refused to take them seriously. So dangerous had the situation become, and so irrational were Fairein's commands, that there was rumour of dissent, and even open rebellion in the forces.

Then came the news that the Vipands had struck in the South. The border towns had been overwhelmed in the first onslaught, and they were advancing across the grasslands, opposed only by the horsemen. Fairein panicked, and ordered all women and children into the Dardane. Even the Sisterhood had been ordered into the stronghold so Dana's link with the events was cut, but the last news she had, seemed to indicate that Fairein was now pulling too many men away from the north, and dangerously depleting the forces holding the Nasdarks at bay.

The three rode day and night. They were well supplied with horses, and pushed the animals to the limits of their endurance, and then turned them loose to make their own way back to water and feed. Some no doubt died of exhaustion or fell to the Firetime Wolves, but no thought could be spared for their suffering.

They rode past the border towns in the deep of night, but there was too much moonlight to save them from the sickening sight of the rows of heads impaled on stakes along all the walls. Most of them were the heads of women and children. The three wept as they rode.

Towards morning, they came upon the trampled wreckage of battle, and were forced to hide all through the hideous day as fighting raged all along the grasslands between them and the Elves. They hid in a small depression, as their remaining horses were in no condition to take them into battle, and there were far too many of their enemies to try to fight a way through. They could not see much of the action, but it was evident that the Elves had been beaten back all through the day with great loss of life.

Night fell at last over the carnage, and the armies pulled back into two giant camps. The three rode cautiously around the Vipands with the Drark scouting ahead. His uncanny ability to see in the night stood them in good stead. Twice, he led them around guard posts, and, where they couldn't skirt the post, he melted into the darkness, and, in a little while, called softly, and they passed through over the silent bodies. So, at last, they came to the Elves, made contact with their outer posts, and eventually were allowed through and taken to a very distraught Descot.

He greeted them wearily. Even though it was near midnight, there were still wounded being tended by too few healers. Only those who had actually defied Fairein's order had stayed to heal. All the rest were in the Dardane, able to supply power but not direct it.

For a while, Dana and the Giant were kept busy healing the most hurt. Many had died, however, for those wounded by poisoned arrow, or poisoned sword blade, had little chance of getting aid in time. Even then, the Sisterhood was at a loss. It had the power to combat the poison if the wound was not too bad, and they got to it soon enough, but they had little previous experience, and it took hours to hold death from one person until the poison dissipated, and the wounded could live unaided.

Later, the Giant urged Descot, who was second in command in the south, to try to get his commander to fall back to the edge of the woods, and to hold the Snakes there, where the trees would give cover, and to some extent negate the advantage the poison gave their foes. He reported that his commander agreed with the strategy, but had been ordered by Fairein not to cede his horse lands to the enemy.

There was little the three could do. Against overwhelming odds, the Elves were sure to suffer terribly next day. The Giant extracted a promise from Descot that he would try to have the less badly wounded evacuated to the woods, and have them try to set up some sort of defensive position so that a defeat on the field might not turn into a rout that would carry the Vipands into the heart of Elfdom. Then the three took fresh horses, and rode on to try to find Fairein, and to determine what was so badly wrong in the Kingdom of the Elves.

They rode through a land that seemed already defeated. Farms were deserted. Domestic animals roamed untended. Crops, and fruit, rotted in fields, and on trees. Large towns were similarly deserted by all except old men, who worked pathetically to build defences that gave only an illusion of security.

They reached the capital, and Alaine, almost at the same time as two messengers. Fairein was at a war council when they arrived. They were waiting to see him when the messengers arrived. The news they carried was devastating. The first brought word that the passes had fallen and the Nasdarks had crossed the Thrul, and were advancing on the capital. The second messenger carried more fatal news. A party of Nasdarks had somehow crossed the Crags of Thane, and had taken the Wolf's Throat. The pass to the Dardane was closed to the Elves. The women and children were in the stronghold, but the way to it was as closed to the Elves as to their foes.

The war council broke up in disarray. There was only one thing the Elves could do. They must try to take the Wolf's Throat before the Nasdarks could reinforce their warriors there, or eventually the Dardane must fall, and the women be destroyed.

Olvar hurried off, shouting orders to raise the guard, and to send messages to all the forces of the Elves to fall back to bar the path to the Dardane. Even the capital was to be sacrificed. In front of the Dardane, the Elves would make their last stand.

Dana rushed off to find Alaine. Midwives briefly barred her path, but retired, deeply affronted, when presented with a naked sword, and given the choice of stepping aside, or dying where they stood. Alaine heard the altercation, and burst out of her apartments, and, though now big with child, ran sobbing into Dana's arms.

Dana quickly told her the situation, and asked what was wrong with Fairein. Alaine tearfully explained that she did not know. She had not been able to speak with him for weeks. He did not even seem to recognise her as his wife much less the mother of his child.

"The Red Queen has him!" Dana declared with terrible conviction. "We've got to get him, and clear his mind." She sent an urgent call to the Giant's mind bidding him waylay Fairein, and hold him until she and Alaine could reach them.

It was not easy. Fairein hardly seemed to recognise the Giant and the Drark. He would have ridden off except Olvar came upon the scene. The Drark hurriedly explained that Alaine had need of her husband. Olvar had come to Vale under the Wood from Alaine's family. He caught Fairein's horse and held it. For a moment, it seemed that Fairein would strike his hand away, but suddenly he went very still. Dana and Alaine came into view. She bonded with the Sisterhood, acquainting them of her conviction that Fairein had fallen victim of the Red Queen, then she drew power from the Giant, and grabbed Fairein's mind.

The struggle was vicious. The Red Queen was there. There were many more behind her, but the sisterhood recognised her mind from the encounter with her Demons in front of Mandanna, and the fury engendered by finding her in the mind of their own Prince sent a surge of hatred through Dana that gave her demonic strength. In a sudden impulse, she clutched at the mind of the Red Queen. There was an instant of surprise, of outrage, of fury, and then fear, and suddenly panic. The Red Queen whipped back. Dana followed along the thread surging after, trying to hold, gripping and losing and gripping again, like a boy trying to hold a struggling eel. Then she lost the thread, and the Red Queen was gone. Fairein reeled and fell into the Olvar's arms. The struggle was not over. He resisted Dana's delving into his mind. But the force she could command left him no power, and she sought beneath his conscious mind and found the vision of Wolverina and the poison she had nightly injected into him. She dragged it all up into the open so he must know it, and all over the land the sisterhood wept for the degradation that their Prince had suffered.

At some time, Fairein began to weep and then to scream. He tried to draw his sword, but Olvar held him tightly, understanding little of what was going on, but aware that the very existence of his species hung in the balance. Then the Sisterhood, under Dana's direction, began the task of healing and bringing peace to Fairein's tortured soul. At last, they had done all they could, and he lay quietly sobbing like a child.

Members of the sisterhood materialised, and Olvar surrendered his Prince to them. Then he looked up at Alaine. "What has happened, Princess?" he asked quietly.

Alaine looked to Dana. The same question in her eyes. "The Red Queen possessed him," she said quietly. "She did it through someone called Wolverina. All his orders since this happened have actually been given by our enemy. No wonder the war is going wrong."

"Is he free of her now?" Alaine asked looking with horror as Fairein was carried away.

"Yes. She's gone, and he knows what was done to him."

"Can she come back? Can she take over his mind again?"

Dana looked even more stricken. "I don't know," she said. "This is new to us. Giant was corrupted by one of her agents, but it was only through the imbedding of a set of false memories that influenced his nature, and would probably have turned him evil. Once we found them, they had no more power. In this case, she has somehow made Fairein sensitive, and was able to take over his mind at will. If he will let us bond with him, we will probably be able to find out how she did it, but it is much to ask a man especially after what he has gone through."

"You did not bond then?"

"No. This is something new also. Giant and I practised it when we thought the Sisterhood was the Red Queen when they were trying to find us for you. We actually grabbed his mind. One can only bond when the other is willing. I was not in Fairein's mind all the time. I tried to hold the Red Queen, and then follow her home. I gave her something of a shock. She'll be less prone to probe here from now on. In the end, she lost me, but I think I know where she is to be found."

Olvar broke in. "What's to be done now? We cannot stand here talking with the Nasdarks at our gates."

Alaine looked at each in turn. "I must take over until we know that Fairein is himself. The Red Queen obviously knows exactly what the situation is. But what can we do? We must get into the Dardane. The army must pull back, and hold the enemy from linking up with those in the Dardane valley or we are lost. I doubt they'll come here first. They know the women are mostly in there, and that is where they'll be going. Olvar you must organise that. Until Fairein is well, you are Commander of our armies. Giant, you and Drark must clear the Wolf's Throat. Dana, you will stay with me. You can keep us in touch with Giant and help with Fairein. We must find a way to keep the Red Queen from him. Olvar, can you think of better plan?"

"No, My Lady. With your permission, I'll away." He barely waited for her nod, and ran off, bellowing commands and calling officers to him.

Chapter 5

Battle

Descot looked out over the bloody grasslands. He wiped a bitter mixture of blood and sweat from his brow, and sadly surveyed the remnants of his command. He tried to ignore the sting of the cut above his eye. He could not remember how he came by it. He did not know if it came from poisoned arrow or equally poisoned sword, or whether some other unfortunate Elf had washed the poison off, whatever it was, with his life's blood. Resolutely he cast it from his mind. If poisoned he was, then he would shortly fall unconscious and die, and that would but bring the inevitable forward a few hours at the most.

He looked back over his shoulder at the pitiful array of a once proud fighting unit. They had ridden in haste from the Northern reaches, and he had commanded them since their commander had died sometime in the last three days. He couldn't remember just when. Word had come from Olvar by way of the Sisterhood to send the entire Third and Fourth strike arms back, and to try to hold the enemy with the Sixth and the remnants of the Seventh. He had done that. When the Sixth had lost their commander, he had incorporated them with his Seventh, and they had fought as a unit.

They had fought well. No one could take that from them. For three days, they had denied their enemies access to the woods and the way into the kingdom, but this was their last stand. They had survived only through the superhuman efforts of the Sisterhood, especially those devoted few, who had refused to obey Fairein's order that they should seek safety in the Dardane, and who had remained to channel the healing power from the Sisterhood, and apparently, all those who had once belonged to the Sisterhood. Men, who would have been mortally wounded in any other nation, were carried back, healed, and returned to fight again. Thus it was, as though the enemy was forced to kill each Elf, again and again, and as their supply of poison seemed to have run short, so could the Sisterhood heal more quickly.

But each wound took its toll, and many died on the field, so now they stood forth for the last time. They were all volunteers. The Healers, and the wounded from the last onslaught, the first for this day, had been sent back to take shelter in the mountains of the Drarks. The Healers were exhausted, and there would be little healing to be done after the next engagement. The Vipands would come again very soon, and this time there just was not enough to throw them back. So Descot had decided to meet them once more on the field, to fight from the back of the steed that he loved, and to die as all true warriors were proud to die, with a sword in his hand and his foe before him. Let the bowmen hold the woods as long as they could, he and his horsemen would fight in the field.

Faintly, he heard the trumpet call on the morning air. His men heard it, too. A ripple like a sigh ran along the ranks. The horses fidgeted a little, and were pulled back into line. Then all became silent and still, as men made their final obeisance to the Gods they thought shortly to meet.

A faint dust rose, and then, over the swell in the land, the long black line of horsemen came, with banners of the Snake streaming above their flashing swords or glinting bows. Descot raised his hand. He wished he had been able to make a decent speech, to tell these men who were about to die with him, how much their valour meant to him, but he had never been good with words. He dropped his hand, and set spurs to his mount, and once more lost control of events, stopped thinking, and let his mind sink below the pound of hoofs about him as his steed carried him into battle.

Arrows and swords, blow for blow, blood for blood, and dead, and dying, and screams, and crying, and Descot found himself in a little knot of men surrounded, unhorsed, back-to-back, and fighting desperately. Horses milled about him. Blades flashed. Twice he saved himself with his sword, and one foe he wounded, and then Elf riders were about him, and the knot had grown, but it still was surrounded. He tried to clamber onto a horse that was suddenly riderless, but it reared and threw him back, but deflected the blade that would have surely killed him. He fell heavily, and for a while all he could see were horses' hooves.

Then there was a sort of stillness. He struggled up and looked for foes. About him were only Elves. All seemed to be like him, wondering where the foe were. They were gone. Descot's head felt light, and objects seemed to swim about him. He wondered if he was dead, and if this stillness belonged to another world. Then someone was holding him up, and offering water, and his head became clearer.

His men were all looking one way, but he couldn't see what they were looking at. *Perhaps a God was coming,* he thought. Then he was helped upon a horse, and he could see. What he saw brought a groan of despair to his lips. He wished he had died, for the Vipands they had been fighting had fallen back, and another black line of warriors had topped the swell, and was racing across the trampled grass on steeds that sped like fire before a wind.

Wearily, Descot lifted his sword. He felt a faint twinge of pride to see the red blood despoiling the gleam of the weapon. He made a swift count. He had about twenty men, most in some way wounded, some without horses. He thought of trying to get back to the woods, but dismissed the thought.

He had known he was going to die. It would be silly to try to delay it. He raised his hand, but he didn't let it fall.

Something was wrong. The Vipands were fighting amongst themselves. Behind the line of riders came another - a strike arm in arrow formation with a strange flag. They cut through the struggling masses of the Vipands and the first line of warriors like a knife through butter, and then the arrow split into two waves that turned as one, and swept around into the backs of the Vipands, crashing through them, and breaking them into milling knots. And now came a third force. A different kind of warrior. Small men on small ponies, that speared into the knots of Vipands, and broke them up so that they fell victim to the circling fighters.

Descot sat stunned. Slowly, he brought his hand down. He looked around at his men, but all looked on as blankly as he. Somehow his foes were being destroyed before his eyes, but he had no idea by whom.

Then a small group of warriors broke away from the battle, and rode towards him at an easy canter. Descot tried to sit straighter, and urged his mount out a little in front of his men. He watched the oncoming warriors closely. They were large men on large horses, but they rode with a peculiar grace unlike other men. They wore thick leather outfits that glinted in the sunlight, probably from studs of steel to form a type of primitive armour, and leather helms through which their own hair streamed out. As they came closer, Descot saw that the leather about the shoulder of their sword arms was cut away to give free swing, and he was astonished to perceive female breasts only lightly clad. These fierce warriors were women.

As they approached, Descot lifted his hand in salute. The leader of the group copied his gesture, and pulled her mount to a stop a few yards from him. "Greetings!" said Descot, "and well met! I know not who you are, but I have much to thank you for. I am Descot, Commander of the Sixth and the Seventh Strike Arms. Who have I to thank for this deliverance?"

"I am Petaine, Commander of this expeditionary force of Femins, Kersh and Bartonians. We seek an Elf warrior, Dana, and her companions, a Giant and a Drark. Do you know of these?"

"But of course! Of course! You are a Femin, a woman warrior. The Sisterhood spoke of you. They got the knowledge from Dana. They are with the Prince as far as I know. I've been busy lately."

Petaine glanced around at the body-littered field, and laughed grimly. "That you have. I am sorry we could not relieve you yesterday. But too few of our forces were here, and we had to clear this vermin out of the towns back there or we would have had Snakes at our backs yet. There will not be many to crawl back to their Snake Queen after this day."

Descot looked past her at the field of battle. Only small groups of Vipands still fought in desperate knots. Even as he watched, a shrill whistle blew, and the warriors about one such group fell back, leaving the Vipands in the middle of a large circle. There was a pause, in which Descot hoped they were given the chance to surrender, and then bowmen stood forth, and a deadly rain of arrows swept the circle clean of all living things. Then the whole group swung towards the next knot. The Vipands were being systematically destroyed.

In some places, however, Vipands had fought free of their encirclers, and were fleeing across the plains with warriors in pursuit. Descot turned back to Petaine. "I had not thought to see such a thing just an hour ago, but if you will forgive this haste, Commander, I have many wounded to see to, and I have sent my healers away. By the Firetime it was an ill decision. I cannot even let the Prince know of this deliverance. I will have to send a messenger." He turned to his men. "Is there any of you unwounded?"

One urged his mount forward, saluting Petaine's group as he did so. "My wounds are but trifles, Sir, and do not appear to be poisoned."

"Go then, Daffid, alert the bowmen to our fortune, and send others off to see if they can find the healers. Bid them return as soon as possible. Then ride you to the Prince." He acknowledged Daffid's salute, and turned back to Petaine.

Petaine smiled grimly. "I shall supply your wounded with the antidote to the Snake's poison. It will at least save some of them. Your warriors fought well by all accounts, and held this vermin against great odds. You also took much of their poison, and made our task much easier. It will be long years before the Snake can threaten our lands again if they survive this day. I will go and see to my warriors and the wounded, and I shall meet with you this night, and tomorrow, with your leave, we will ride to find Dana."

She turned her mount, and her warriors turned in unison, and soon they were galloping back across the grass, their mounts lightly jumping the many bodies lying about. With the need to hide his pain and weariness gone, Descot slumped, and his men quickly came to his side. "Let us go," he said. "We have been delivered, but I'm too tired to cheer, and too numb to celebrate. Let us tend to the wounded, and thank the Gods for this day." He smiled suddenly. "Just think of the Nasdarks' faces when women ride down on them like that." He then slid unconscious from his mount.

Chapter 6

Urdrill the Drark

The Giant turned to the Drark as Dana left, supporting Alaine. "What's the Wolf's Throat?" he asked.

The Drark chuckled. "The pass that is impossible to take," he said.

"Impossible! I don't like the sound of that, Drark. Why impossible?"

"Because of its nature. At least that was what the Elves thought. But it is obvious they were wrong because the Nasdarks have taken it. Who do you think this Wolverina is?"

"An agent of the Red Queen obviously, and a pretty effective one to seduce Fairein. She is, no doubt, in contact with her mistress, and so we had better take steps to have her isolated, especially from Fairein. I'll get Dana to bond with the Sisterhood in the Dardane and see to it."

He went still for a few moments, and then relaxed. "She's doing it." He said. Then he stiffened, listening. "We're too late. Wolverina has just been thrown off the walls of the Dardane stronghold by the women. According to Dana we wouldn't have been able to save her even if we had been there. Apparently she was the cause of the loss of the Wolf's Throat. It seems she had been in the habit of visiting the guard posts at night, and making love with the sentries. It is thought she visited them one by one, and knifed them. Then the Nasdarks, who must have come through the mountains, just walked in and took over. There's not a great number of them, but they are supposed to be a prime arm. They attacked those working in the valley, but failed to take the Stronghold, so most of the women and children are safe for some time. It seems they have been content to hold the Wolf's Throat believing that their comrades will be able to fight through, and link up with them. Then they can move into the Dardane in force, and hold the Elves from relieving the Stronghold. Eventually those in it will have to surrender or starve to death. The women will die either way. That is apparently why the Red Queen had Fairein order all the women into it. It is a giant trap. He even did his best to get Alaine to go. I wonder if he knew what he was doing? Surely not!"

"You are right, there, Giant. I know Fairein well enough to know that he would have killed himself before he gave such orders. This is a new, and deadly, ability of the Red Queen. Imagine if she had been able to so possess your mind, Giant, when her agent had access to you. I wonder if she then could not do so, or did not consider you important enough to spend the time. Surely it would have to be a constant thing possessing someone else's mind. It bears thinking on, for, if her powers are still growing, then we needs must destroy her the sooner, or the Gods alone know what we'll face in the future. But now this Wolf's Throat. I cannot imagine how these Nasdarks crossed the mountains unless they were given leave, and aid, by Mandrill who still rules, I believe. How they would have got that, I have no way of knowing. I wonder if the Drarks have an agent amongst them also. But then the Drarks do not take in strangers. How would one get to them? It is perhaps time I went home, Giant."

"Home? Drark? Are you not outcast?"

"Outcast, yes. But not to the death. Mandrill, himself, I have no quarrel with, but with his son, the Prince. If I can get to Mandrill, I can perhaps find how these Nasdarks crossed our lands, and, if they got not leave from him, then he will be displeased with them indeed."

"And what if the Prince now rules?"

"Then I'll die."

"What if you run into him before you get to Mandrill? Even if Mandrill still rules?"

"Then one of us will probably die. It would be useless going before Mandrill then, should I be the survivor."

"If Mandrill does still rule, and you find out how the Nasdarks got through his lands, how does that help us clear the Wolf's Throat? It seems wasted effort to me, Drark. Better to ride to the Dardane, and see if we can fight our way in."

"Not so, Giant. The Elves were quite right. It is impossible to take the Wolf's Throat when competent warriors properly guard it, and you can be assured that the Nasdarks are that. I have seen it. As great a fighter as you are, Giant, you will not take it. Your size, in itself, would be to your disadvantage. You could not swing your blade in there even if you got through the arrows they would fire at you. No. There is only one way to clear the Nasdarks from the Wolf's Throat, and that is to get Drarks to do it. If Mandrill is annoyed enough he may give me the men to do it."

"How are Drarks so needed? If it is too narrow for me, why not use Elves? Surely they could fight in there, and there are mighty fighters amongst the Elves, as I saw outside Mandanna."

"I have no criticism of Elves as warriors, Giant, but Drarks have one great advantage over Elves in fighting in the Wolf's Throat, and over Nasdarks, too. They see where others cannot. Wolverina took the Wolf's Throat by night using her body. So, too, would the Drarks, using their eyes."

The Giant shrugged. "So be it. Let us ride to your home, and this time I'll guard your back."

The Drark smiled grimly. "I well may need that service. But let us eat and rest first, and then find fresh horses. It is a rough ride into the mountains."

In that, he was not wrong, as the Giant found. It was seven weary days of almost continuous riding that brought them into a wide, thickly wooded valley deep in the Western Mountains beyond the borders of the elfin realm.

"Now we find who reigns in the halls of Drarkenland," the Drark said grimly. He drew his mount to a halt outside the entrance of a fairly unremarkable cave in the side of a cliff near where a stream fell in a mighty cascade from the heights into the valley.

The Giant looked round. Apart from a faint track in the rocky ground, there was nothing to indicate that it was more than a mere den of mountain bears or Firetime wolves. "This is an entrance to a...a city, Drark?"

"One of them. We have been watched since yesterday. They expect us to ride to the end of the valley. There they will have a reception waiting for us. It will not be friendly, even if Mandrill still lives."

"Will they not have watchers here also?"

"It is possible. I'm hoping they have not recognised me. Drarks do not see at all well in the sunlight, and I was very careful to stay hidden last night. If they think I am not a Drark, they will not have this way guarded, for only a Drark could enter here."

"You see well enough in sunlight. Why not your fellows?"

"I was forced into sunlight as a child. It is a strange idea for other people to hear, Giant, but Drarks hide in the sunlight. The brighter the day, the less likely they are to be found. It is night that holds the fear of discovery for us, for Drarks walk the outside world at night."

They had dismounted and tied their mounts in a dense thicket. Then they stole into the cave, and the Giant was soon blind. The Drark seemed not to be discomforted by the darkness, however. He took the Giant's hand, and led him quickly along narrow passages, past openings from which faint air drafts stirred, over stone bridges from which their footsteps echoed hollowly, and through small clefts that had the Giant squirming.

As they rested after one such struggle, the Giant whispered, "How do even you see, Drark? We must be miles from any light."

"We are," replied his companion, "but there is a fungus growing on the walls. We plant it and tend it. It gives off a light invisible to you, but enough to let us see. We call it Travelglow."

After another half hour of travel, they came suddenly on a large cave dimly lit by another type of fungus. People moved about the floor of the cave, and the walls were pocked with openings into and out of which people came. "What is this?" the Giant whispered.

"The outskirts of the city, a poorer part. I have friends here, or, at least, I did have. Stay here. Your size cannot but be noticed. I'll go and find out what has passed since I left." The Drark indicated a dark corner out of view of the cave. "Remember they can see much better than you," he said, and suddenly seemed to vanish into the semi darkness.

The Giant sat down, glad enough of the chance to rest, but unhappily aware of the darkness, and the mass of rock between him and the outside world. Time passed very slowly. The rocks he sat upon became harder, and sharper. They pressed the fine mesh of his mail into his flesh. There was neither sun nor stars to give him an indication of the passing of time. He risked peeping into the inhabited cave. There seemed less people about, but that was the only difference. He wondered if he could contact Dana through the rock. He tried. There was a great blankness about him.

Then he touched a mind, or thought he did. Quickly he withdrew, closing his awareness tightly. Then he sat and pondered. It had been so strange a mind that he was not sure if it was human. At last curiosity overcame his caution, and he cast out gently again. He found the mind, seeking eagerly, questing with a terrible intenseness. Once more he withdrew, and, in doing so, felt a fierce cry of pain and of loss. The mind had to be human. He supposed it had to be that of a Drark, but it seemed to have the attributes of a caged animal struggling to escape some captivity, desperately seeking awareness and knowledge.

He felt a desire to seek and comfort that forlorn being, but too much hinged on the success of the Drark's mission to do anything that might lead to their premature discovery. So he waited. Hours passed. The Drark had been gone too long. Worry began to gnaw at the Giant's mind. He knew that he had no way of finding his way out of the caves.

Then suddenly the Drark was beside him. He slipped in and silently handed over a sort of vegetable and meat loaf and a fresh container of water. Only then did the Giant realise how hungry he was. As he ate, the Drark spoke in a low voice. "Our cause is lost. Mandrill still reigns, but Urdrill rules."

"Urdrill?"

"The Prince. Apparently, Mandrill was wounded in an assassination attempt. He has lost his sight. Urdrill has taken over. It's rumoured that he was behind the attempt. No one is able to get in to see Mandrill. Urdrill's men supply the guard."

"Could we fight our way in?"

"We could probably get in all right. I doubt if they would be expecting an attack, but if Mandrill has not the power to take back his rule, then we would be doomed. Once Urdrill is roused, we would never get back out of the palace."

"What then to do?"

"None that offers much hope, me thinks. We can leave the way we came, and try to clear the Wolf's Throat ourselves. Or we can risk all on Mandrill. I still think only Drarks can clear the pass, and we run the risk of many more Nasdarks getting through the mountains into the Dardane. I think it best if I try to get to Mandrill by stealth. You are too big, and too noticeable, to try anything in here by stealth. I'll lead you back out to the cave we entered. Then

I'll try to get in to Mandrill. If it is true he is being held against his will, and if he is willing to help us, then I'll come and get you, or send someone. We'll break him out to loyal warriors, and challenge Urdrill. By the way the people are talking in this area at least, they'll be pleased enough to see the last of Urdrill. If you do not hear from me by sunrise tomorrow, then I've been taken. Go you then, and try to take the Wolf's Throat with Elves."

It was early evening when they reached the mouth of the cave. With a whispered warning to be alert to the fact that Drark patrols were out at night, and a tight handclasp to mark what might be their last parting, the Drark slipped back into the darkness. The Giant made his way carefully down to the thicket wherein they had hidden the horses, and saw to their comfort. Then he returned to the mouth of the cave, and settled down in its hidden recesses to wait the night away.

He slept only fitfully. No Drark came to call him. The sky grew inexorably paler. Dawn broke. The sun rose. The Drark or his messenger did not come. There was little the Giant could do. He could not storm the citadel of the Drarks. He could not even find it without aid. He decided to wait about two hours, and then he would have to leave to give himself enough daylight to clear the valley, and enough of the mountains to be relatively free of pursuit. Then he decided that, when the business of the Elves and the Red Queen was over, he would return, and try to find out the fate of his friend, and free him or avenge his death.

He waited. No word came. Just before his appointed time was up, he remembered the forlorn mind that he had been forced to abandon. There seemed little danger in contacting it again. Even if he was discovered, it seemed that in daylight the Drarks would be no match for him even if they attacked in numbers. He sat down with his sword naked to hand, and cast his mind back into the cave. At first he encountered only the blankness of thick rock, but then he closed his eyes, and tried to send his mind down the labyrinth of caves and tunnels he and the Drark had traversed. The mind, when he found it, was half drugged with sleep, but suddenly it burst clear of the mists in a brilliant flash of excitement that turned swiftly to entreaty. "Don't go! Please don't leave me! Who are you? I need you so! Oh, please don't turn off! Are you one of the Elf sisterhood? I have heard of the Sisterhood. You do not feel like a woman. You feel male. Are you a man? You are not a Drark? Who and what are you? Please answer! Can you answer? Oh, Firetime! Am I dreaming only?"

"I can answer. I am male, but not a man. I am Giant, though the Giants say no. Who are you, and why this desperate need for mind touch? Most people are little eager to touch the mind of strangers."

"I am Lalona. I broke the bones of my neck in a fall. I cannot move nor speak. I have lain these long years in terrible darkness of the mind. I was a princess. Now I am nothing. A plaything for a cruel Prince to mock. He takes his pleasure from my body, and exults when I cannot hide the hate in my eyes. Will you help me to escape him?"

"Is the Prince you speak of Urdrill?"

"Yes! May the Firetime return and burn his flesh for a thousand years! You are not friend of Urdrill. I can feel it."

"No, I am not friend of Urdrill. Have you heard of the bonding the Sisterhood do?"

"Yes, though I know not what it is exactly."

"Your mind is very clear. I think I can bond with you. It is a sharing of mind and memory. For a while we will be one being, our minds will be one. It is a terrible thing to ask of you, but it is the only way I can be sure of the truth of your words. I am a friend of a Drark called Pen who has been outcast from here, and who has returned to try to see your King. It seems he has failed. Now I must soon leave, for there is much strife in the realm of the Elves. If we do this thing, then I shall know you, and all your history, all your joys and sorrows, and likewise you will know mine. Much is very private, and I would never ask of it without great need."

"What must I do?"

"Just remain calm, and do not fight the intrusion as one instinctively does."

"I can do that. It will be far more welcome an intrusion then the shaft of Urdrill."

The bond came very easily. After an initial fright, Lalona suddenly realised the wealth of experience, and of knowledge of the world, that was open to her. Her mind blazed with delight, and flashed from memory to memory like a butterfly. The Giant sighed as he gently broke contact. He knew he could not go, and leave any women in the situation this Princess suffered. She knew him well enough even after so short a bonding to realise that also, but now she knew the plight of the Elves, and the loss of Pen.

For a little while, Lalona's mind stayed in turmoil but then she made a very conscious effort and gained control. "That is an experience I never dreamed possible, Giant. I would bond with you again and again, but I see your need for haste. Poor Pen. I fear you are right, and he must be taken. Urdrill will surely kill him if he is not already done so. He is my half-brother as you probably now know, and once I loved him dearly. Do you know? How much of me do you know? There is so much of you. So much you have done, and Rachel and Dana. Oh, how you love Dana. Would someone ever love me so much, and she knows it. You bond, and she knows how much you love her--what a wonderful thing, but how awful if your love faded--she would know. Could I bear that? But I ramble. You think you and Dana might be able to help me...cure me. Is that possible?"

"I do not know. It is possible enough to be worth trying. This Urdrill is truly an evil man. He should be brought down. How can I get to you?"

"I can lead you. I know where you are. I know those paths well. Pen and I used to play there. We would sneak outside when all slept, for both of us have suneyes. It was lucky for him that he had, when Urdrill him made outcast. Come to me now. It is day outside, and all here are asleep. There is one of my maids, called Sonta, with whom I can communicate by eye movements. She is good and reliable. I'll send her to guide you to me once you get to the city. Come now - move to the back of the cave, and take the first crevice to the right ..."

It took almost two hours to get through the caves and tunnels. Once the Giant missed a turning, and followed instructions until he ran up against a blank wall before they realised that he had gone wrong. Then he had to feel about in the dark for some time until he touched a thin trickle of water, and was able to follow it up until it dropped over three tiny falls. Lalona then knew where he was, and was able to redirect him. Her recollection of the ways were little short of miraculous, but still the Giant would have suffered badly had it not been for his mail and gauntlets, as her concept of his size was far from accurate, and she sent him into crevices and tunnels that were too small for him, and he had to squeeze and crawl. Still, after the two hours, he suddenly saw light, and made out the slim figure of a Drark waiting in the shadows.

Then followed a tense traverse of much of the city, made possible only by the Giant's knowledge of its ways and by-ways, gained from the mind of Lalona. The girl sped ahead, spotting patrols and signalling the Giant into hiding or into lanes cut between houses that led him around the danger. A couple of late revellers chanced to see him, and with hoarse cries of fear, bolted into a public house that was still open and well patronised, if the noise stemming from it was used in judgement. Their wild description must have met with disbelief, for only guffaws of laughter came back out, as the Giant and the girl crept past. It was the best part of another hour before they reached a wealthier looking part of the city, where the houses were delved into the stone of the mountain itself, and rose three or four storeys above the level of the cave. Here, ornate windows and balconies, all hung with the fluorescent fungus, that the Giant's newly acquired memories from Lalona enabled him to identify as lightglow. It was into one of these that Sonta eventually drew the Giant, and he could once more breathe easily.

He was brought immediately into the presence of Lalona. She lay on a slightly slanting bed, piled with cushions, and covered by a thin silken sheet. A strong perfume clogged the air of the room. The Giant stood, towering over the bed, looking down at the slim body before him. The face that stared up at him was immobile. Only the large, black, Drarken eyes moved, and shone with excitement. "Thank the Gods that you got here," she said into his mind. "Can you help?"

"I do not know, Princess," the Giant answered. "I am not a healer in my own right. I supply only the power for Dana to heal. However, if I can get you outside where I can bond with Dana then perhaps she can heal you from a distance. It is worth trying. Can we reach the outside? Your memory is of a place near here."

"Yes. There is a balcony at the back of the house that overlooks the outside. It is from there that I was pushed." Anger coloured her thoughts. "You must carry me there."

"That I can do, but I fear I am in no condition to be so close to a maiden. It is days since I have had the chance to bathe."

Lalona's mind flickered with amusement. "Think you I am any better? I have lost control of my body functions. That is the reason for the perfume that had you wrinkling your nose, Giant. Let me tell you, that without it, you would be wrinkling it far more. If you can put up with me, then I can surely stand the honest smell of toil and travel."

The Giant shrugged, and stooped to gather the thin body and lifted it away from the bed. Lalona was naked under the sheet so he hurriedly wrapped it around her. Then he turned to Sonta who had been hovering in the background, completely at a loss as to what was happening. "Lead me to the balcony that is on the outside of the mountain," he commanded. The girl hesitated, but a series of eye movements from her mistress sent her scurrying through the door, beckoning him to follow.

In a few minutes, heavy drapes were pushed aside, and the Giant walked, blinking, into bright sunshine. Sonta could not keep her eyes open but still tried to follow. The Giant sent her back to bring cushions, and then gently lowered his charge onto the hard, stone floor. Then he sent out an urgent call for Dana. He was answered almost immediately, and she came swiftly into his mind. A few moments were all that was necessary for her to be apprised of the situation and the need to cure Lalona.

It was a novel experience for both of them, and only possible because they had bonded so often that they had acquired the ability to merge minds so fully that each could use the other's senses. Dana could look down through the Giant's eyes, and could use his mind and body as an almost perfect channel for her own. The Giant, for his part, could relax his control, and concentrate only on supplying power. Thus it was Dana's mind that blocked pain from the mind of the patient. It was her mind that guided the Giant's fingers to bear pressure on the broken bones of the neck, and to take his knife and delicately cut through the flesh, and about the bones so that they could be brought into place, and forced to knit whole once more. Then it was her art that stopped the flow of blood and caused the wounds to heal.

It took the best part of three hours, and the Giant was starting to feel the effects of supplying so much mind power, before Dana was satisfied, and gently released the princess from her mind hold. Lalona opened her eyes and smiled. Then she slowly lifted a hand and looked at it. The Giant reached down and lifted her upright. The sheet fell from her body, but she ignored it. She lifted both arms up, and stretched to her full height, and uttered a great cry of glee. Sonta burst through the heavy drapes holding a hand before her eyes, and desperately groping for her mistress.

Lalona caught her in her arms, and swung her round so vigorously that the Giant hastily stepped between them, and the edge of the balcony. He gently touched Lalona's mind with a plea for caution, and she immediately sobered. "You are right, Giant Peter. I like Peter best. Come Sonta, go and get me some clothes. I am not altogether shameless. Oh! But what is nakedness to being able to move and talk?" She swung Sonta in through the drape, and sent the bemused maid on her way with a caution to tell no one of the miracle. Then she turned to the Giant. "We must get to Mandrill. If you can cure him, he will fight Urdrill and take his Kingdom back. We can get along the side of the mountain here. There is a path, dangerous, but less so than trying the doors of the palace. Urdrill would have me killed on sight."

The Giant nodded. "Bond with me a moment and show me this path. I have only hazy knowledge of it from last time."

They bonded for a moment or two while Lalona followed the path in her mind. They broke contact. "That is how I remember it," Lalona said. "It was a long time ago that I last went that way."

"It is good enough. Will it be guarded, think you?"

"Not the outside. But inside the balcony it probably will be to prevent anyone getting in to Mandrill."

"Then we must destroy the guard without raising the house. I wish we had Pen. He was good at things like that."

Sonta returned carrying a bundle of clothes. Lalona discarded most, and pulled on a simple dress. "Come. The hours of sleep are slipping away, and we need to cure Mandrill before the waking."

Sonta was sent to take word to a trusted friend of Lalona's who was a known enemy of Urdrill's. Then Lalona and the Giant started the dangerous traverse of the mountain face. The way was thankfully not far, and in little more than ten minutes they dropped lightly onto another balcony. The Giant quietly drew his sword, and slipped in behind the heavy drapes that shut the daylight out of the corridor. He stood for a minute or so letting his eyes grow used to the pale glow of glowlight. Then the two crept silently forward, Lalona's mind guiding the Giant round obstacles on the floor.

They found the guard half asleep. There were only three Drarks. The Giant moved with deadly swiftness. Two died before they were fully aware of the attack. The third jumped to his feet, and got his sword drawn but the Giant's blade swept it aside and took half his throat with it. He gurgled his way to the floor, and the silence returned. They crept on.

There were no more guards, and they entered Mandrill's quarters. A page boy scrabbled out of his bedclothes at the foot of Mandrill's bed, and opened his mouth to scream, but the Giant's hand closed round his neck, and he was lifted up, and hung dangling with bulging eyes. It was lucky for him that Lalona recognised him. She stopped the Giant with a whispered word, and took control of the shivering child as the Giant went to Mandrill, who had been awakened by the disturbance. Lalona joined him, still holding the boy. "Hush, Lord," she whispered. "It is I, Lalona. We come to cure your sight."

"Lalona? Lalona? What foolishness is this? Lalona lies more crippled than I. Kill me, if that is your orders, but take me not for a fool."

"Hush, Uncle. It is truly I. I have been healed by this Giant and the healer of the Elves. If you will let us, we will heal you, and help you regain your throne."

"Regain my throne. Yes. I would like to do that. Tell me. Is Urdrill as foul as he boasts to me he is?"

"More foul, I think, Uncle. He oppresses your people terribly."

"And you, child? He says he toys with you?"

"He has used my body weekly. Ever since he had me pushed over the balcony. Helpless victims give him most pleasure."

"Yes. He gloats on my helplessness. I think it is you. No one else would speak as you do. I doubt if you can bring sight to these eyes of mine, but go ahead and try. I have nothing to lose, and much to gain."

The Giant took his arm, and lifted him from the bed. Lalona guided them both back out to the balcony. The boy squawked in fright at the sight of the dead men in the guardroom. Mandrill stopped and sniffed. "I smell fresh blood," he said.

"They had a guard," said the Giant.

Mandrill chuckled. "I'm beginning to enjoy this dream," he said.

They reached the balcony, and settled the King down on the hard floor. Once more, Dana came into the Giant's mind, and he turned strangely gentled fingers to the King's head. It was a fairly simple procedure. A head wound had put pressure on the optic nerve. It took some effort to release the pressure, but it was easy then for Dana to repair the nerve. In a little while they were forced to help the king into the mouth of the passage as the light was hurting his suddenly sensitive eyes. He stood looking about him, and blinking, and then turned to the Giant and Lalona.

"We need men," he said straightening his body, and looking once more a King of his people.

"I've sent for Dontree. He is the only one I'm sure of. He'll bring men, if he believes the message."

Mandrill nodded. "No matter what happens, I thank you for doing this. If I regain my throne, my thanks will be more practical. Now tell me all that has passed."

Lalona sat on the side of the bed, and began to tell of the evil of Urdrill and his reign of terror. She spoke for some time telling of the coming, and apparent capture, of Pen, and of her contact with the mind of the Giant. At last, she was interrupted by the Giant who lifted his fingers to his lips in a signal for silence. "Someone comes," he whispered, drawing his sword and motioning the other two back. Three men stepped warily into the room also with drawn swords. Lalona gave a little cry of gladness, and stepped around the Giant. "It is Dontree. Well met, dear friend."

The leader of the group uttered an incredulous gasp. "It is truly Lalona! Princess! And on your feet again. This is a fortune unlooked for indeed. I believed the girl quite mad. And my Lord - you see again! What miracle has done this thing?"

"I do indeed see again, good Dontree. The miracle comes from the art of the Elves, I am told, channelled through this new friend of ours, who seems to slay foes and heal friends, with equal skill. We have much to thank him for already. I thank you, too, for your faith, Dontree. It'll not be forgotten. But are two warriors the best you can do to aid us? We have need of many."

"Not so, Lord. I left twenty men outside. I feared a trap. Your son has tried to trap me before. I escaped only by good fortune. I did not wish to bring good men down with me. I can get them in a moment. What are your orders?"

"Orders? I have no orders. I have no plan. Until almost this moment I thought me in a dream, and I would waken to the infernal dark. But plan we must. The first is simple. We must take the palace, and let not Urdrill know as long as possible. Then we must hold it. You must send word to all we can trust. Lalona has told me that Pen is in the city, probably held captive by Urdrill if he has not been killed. If he still lives, and we could rescue him, the waverers will flock to him. He could always better Urdrill, and the people know it."

Lalona broke in. "I must go home. Urdrill will come this waking. He will come to abuse me and to gloat. I know he will. It has ever been his way. If he has some news that will hurt me, he tells me as he uses my body. I cannot disguise the pain in my eyes, and it gives him great pleasure. I think it is the only reason he has allowed me to live. He will come, and he will tell me about Pen. If he is still alive, he will tell me so, for he'll have some reason for keeping him alive. He may even say where he has him held. I can contact Peter's mind, and let him know. When he comes in, he locks the doors behind him before he takes off his clothes and his mail, for he does not trust his own men. If we can keep word of the King's healing from him, then he may be taken in my room, and the struggle for the throne will be far less."

"It will be very dangerous for you, Princess," demurred Dontree. "Will you not take men to hide, and be ready to defend you should he realise that you are healed?"

"You do not have men to spare, Dontree. The King must be protected above all else. For, if he dies, then Urdrill automatically becomes King, and all must bow before him. Besides, I do not know when he will come. If someone escapes from here, and warns Urdrill before we have gathered enough of our people, then he will seal off the palace, and you will all die when victory is within our reach. Nothing would suit him better than to have an excuse to destroy you, and be able to slay the king and blame it on you. No. It is better that I undertake this alone. Urdrill must suspect nothing. If he comes to me, then he will be isolated from news. He is ever afraid of assassination. He has his men search thoroughly. Then they go off, and abuse my servants as he abuses me. The doors to my rooms are locked, and he will admit no one while he is undressed. He has threatened to bring all the members of my household in, one by one, and put them to the sword in front of me, if there is any sign of treachery. Should he find hidden soldiers, he would do that and then kill me, and we would not learn news of Pen. No. Once I get the news of Pen from him, then you may come, and take the house. I must hope he tells me of Pen when first he comes, but I fear I must suffer before he does."

"So be it, Princess," said Dontree. "You have great courage, and I wish you well. I do not understand how you will be able to let this Giant know from so far away that Urdrill has come to you, but I have seen enough wonders this day to accept another on faith. Be you assured that as soon as we know if Pen is alive or dead, we'll come, and smash down the doors. Let us hope that you are still alive when we do so."

***

Lalona lay on the hard massage table, and resolutely kept her body relaxed and flaccid. She was lucky in that the two women who worked to tone her muscles had gossip to impart, one to the other, and took little notice of her, save to ensure that she was not bruised. They worked for Urdrill, who commissioned them to keep Lalona's body as fit and as beautiful as possible, not for any concern for her well-being, but for his own pleasure when he raped her. Once, one of them had bruised her thigh badly, and they had not been able to disguise it. Urdrill had each of his bodyguards abuse the unfortunate women, and then had killed her brutally with his own sword. Since then, Lalona had suffered no more bruises.

At last, they were done, and her own servants were allowed to bathe and perfume her body. It was strange after so long to feel the water on her skin, but she could not afford to let even so loyal servants as these know of her cure, lest one should inadvertently let Urdrill become aware that something was different.

Then came the news that she both hoped for, and dreaded. Urdrill had come. She watched him come into the room sword in hand as always, and accompanied by a dozen soldiers. She listened to the noise the men made as they searched her rooms, but could only see Urdrill as he stood in front of her leering down. Then before his men left, he did something he had never done before. He casually lifted the cover off her with his sword, and invited his men to look upon her beauty. They crowded around leering and grinning. He discussed her body with them as though she was some type of animal. Then, when he tired of humiliating her in that way, he sent them off with the injunction to find women of their own. They crowded out, laughing and jesting coarsely. Urdrill stood at the door until the first screams marked their finding of their quarry. Then he closed and locked the door, and walked to the end of the bed, standing at her feet and gazing sardonically down upon her. It was a bed, or rather a platform, that he had had specially constructed. Its height had been carefully measured, and it had a deep indentation in the end so that her legs had to be widely spread to remain on it, and he could walk up between them bringing his penis to her vagina while he stood erect. It slanted upwards at an angle sufficient to allow him to watch her eyes as he stood there.

She watched with sinking heart while he slowly stripped his mail and clothing from his body. He said nothing to her. Panic threatened to overcome her. She did not know if she could bear to suffer his rape without reacting, and yet he had said nothing of Pen. The Giant knew he was there, and men were on their way, but they could do nothing until he told her of Pen.

At last he spoke. "Good morning, Princess. As beautiful and as silent as ever, I see. That is how I like my women. Silent. Except for the odd scream when I enter them. I like to hear them scream then. It is a great shame you cannot scream." He laughed, and ran his hands roughly up along her inner thighs spreading her legs even further. It took all her will power to stop from reacting. He saw the struggle in her eyes, and laughed. He read her horror at his touch, and it excited him sexually as it always did. His penis swelled, and stiffened, and he swept his hand down to project it out from his body, and thrust it brutally into her. Her body was thrust up the slant of the platform, then slid back as he withdrew only to thrust again. She managed to keep from screaming, and the violent impacts and his excitement, stopped him from recognizing the reactions she could not avoid. At last he flooded into her, and the violent battering eased off and stopped. Tears ran from her eyes in silent weeping. He stood with his hands on her hips bent over resting. "You are getting better, my dear. That was very good. And because you were so good I've got a present for you. Look who's come to visit." He laughed, and swaggered over to the door.

He unlocked it, and dragged something in. Then she heard him relock the door, and approach the bed dragging something. "He's not very pretty, my dear. But then Pen was never very pretty, were you, Pen?" He laughed again, and lifted his burden high. It was Pen. Viciously bound and gagged, but clearly Pen, and alive. He was still laughing as he dragged Pen into the indentation between her legs. "Have a good look, Pen. Beautiful, isn't she? I have just enjoyed her. I'm going to do so again. It will be even better this time because I'm going to kill you here in front of her, and killing people like you excites me. She's going to hate that, Pen, and that excites me, too. Always a favourite of the Princess, weren't you? And look here, Lalona. Pen has brought you a present. His sword. Remember when he won it, and you presented it to him? It should have been mine you know. He cheated. I should have won, but he had to win everything. Just to make me look small in the eyes of the people. Well, I don't look small now do I? I'm going to kill him with his own sword, but after he watches me enjoy you. This is a wonderful day. Look, I'm ready for you again." He thrust his huge hips forward, and laughed with pride as he displayed his penis, engorged and erect again. He laid the sword across her breasts to clasp her about the waist and pull her violently towards him as he thrust into her again. Thrice he thrust, and then he looked back over his shoulder to gloat at his prisoner. "Enjoying this, Pen. I am .."

Lalona's control broke. With both hands she grabbed the sword and struck. Urdrill felt her body move. For all his bulk, and great belly, he was quick as a mountain cat. He shoved her away as he sprang back. The blade, inexpertly and awkwardly swung, missed his throat, but gashed his shoulder. Surprise, pain, and rage warred for control of his features. He roared like a feral bull and drew back his fist to smash into Lalona's face, but she sprang from the bed, bringing the sword up, and he saw his danger. Her defiance infuriated him even more, and with another savage roar, he sprang for his own sword. He came up grinning evilly as he crouched into a swordsman's stance, and began to advance on the girl. She retreated round behind the platform, her mind in a frenzy. Suddenly the Giant's mind was with hers. "Bond! Bond!" it demanded, and, with the first hint of understanding, the bond came, just as Urdrill leapt upon the platform, and swung down with a mighty stroke. Lalona's sword came up in a twisting stroke. It did not try to stop the blow but deflected it past her body, and continued in a darting thrust that slashed into Urdrill's inner right thigh, and swept upward towards his naked genitals. He saved them only by throwing himself backwards off the platform.

He was twice wounded now, and blood was flowing freely from both wounds. Caution began to dampen his rage. He turned to the door. Lalona darted around ahead of him, and her sword barred his way. He stared at her in surprise, while outside on the balcony, soldiers, loyal to Mandrill, stared in amazement as the Giant, who had been leading them in a race to get to Lalona, now stood with sword defying passage to a phantom opponent. That Lalona should actually defy him with a sword was a concept Urdrill found hard to accept. She, who had long been his helpless victim, now threatened him with her pitiful strength. The sword was far too heavy for her slim arm, yet she had twice wounded him. She had dared to strike him, and the wounds stung and bled. Rage once more banished caution, and he rushed forwards, raining blow upon blow against the girl. Her sword deflected the blows while her body twisted and turned, but was forced further, and further, back. At last she was trapped in a corner of the room, and could retreat no further. Triumph flooded Urdrill's face. "Die, you Bitch!" he screamed, and lifted his sword with both hands to its greatest height. He had forgotten that he wore no mail. Lalona's foot kicked against the wall, propelling her into a dive with sword outstretched. The blade drove deeply into Urdrill's stomach just above the navel, while Lalona released it, hit the floor, and rolled swiftly away so that Urdrill's blade struck fire from the stone where she had been. She came lithely to her feet and faced him.

His face had turned grey. Shock had widened his eyes. He opened his mouth to roar, but blood choked him. He dropped his own sword, and put both hands to the hilt of Lalona's, and, with a convulsive heave, drew it from his body and threw it from him. Blood spurted massively from the wound and entrails bulged out of it. With a burbling cry, he clasped both hands to the gaping wound trying to push the entrails back in and stem the flood. Realisation of his condition showed in his eyes. A terrible fear contorted his face as he recognised his death. He tried to say something, but no words came. Slowly he sank to his knees. With a great effort he tried to rise again, but he had not the strength. He began to crawl towards the girl. His rage was gone. There was entreaty in his eyes now. He was begging for help. She stepped back, then, when the Giant broke the bond, turned and fled from him. She rushed to Pen's side, and began feebly plucking at his bonds. Urdrill managed to turn towards them before he sank to the floor, and lay writhing feebly in a widening pool of blood.

With a crash, the door behind them burst open, and the Giant sprang into the room with questing blade. He was just in time. There were sounds of fighting on the stairs, and the door to the main part of the house was being hammered. It, too, burst open, and three of Urdrill's men rushed in. They propped, trying to take in the situation. They, too, had been surprised in the act of rape, and wore no mail. The Giant sprang forward. His size stunned his opponents. The foremost lifted his sword only to have it smashed against his body as the Giant's blade crashed through it before scything his body in two. The other two stared in horror for an instant, then turned and fled. The sound of battle increased, and then came abruptly to a halt. Dontree rushed into the room, and halted on the blood-slicked floor only just in time to prevent himself being impaled on the Giant's sword. He grinned savagely as his eyes swept the room, and fastened on Urdrill. The Giant went over, and flicked the bonds from Pen with his sword, and swept the gag from his mouth. "Well met, Drark!" he said, as he picked up a sheet and wrapped it around the shivering girl.

Pen spat a couple of times, and swallowed convulsively. "You could have got here quicker, Giant," he reproved mildly.

The Giant laughed. "Others seem to have done well enough. How fair you, Lady?"

Lalona's body shivered violently despite the warmth of the room. She found it difficult to speak, and only shook her head. Sonta came in, holding the remnants of torn clothing about her body. At the sight of her mistress, she uttered a little cry of distress and ran forward. The two women clasped each other, and sobbed. Other servants began to gather round, staring in amazement at their mistress. Dontree addressed them. "Princess Lalona is suffering a great deal of shock. Conduct her to another room and bring her wine."

The men stood silently while the women departed. Then Dontree turned to Urdrill. He reached down and clutched a handful of hair, and dragged Urdrill into a sitting position. Urdrill's eyes opened. He was still alive, but barely so. Dontree turned to one of his men. "You had a sister, I believe?" he said holding Urdrill's head up at arm's length.

The man's eyes widened, then he nodded. "That I did, Lord," he said, and swung his sword with both hands. There was a slight slapping sound, and Urdrill's body slumped back onto the floor while Dontree held his head high.

"Put that on a pike, and take it to the front of the palace, and then through the streets. It will stop the fighting, but don't take it near Mandrill. He was, after all, the King's son." He turned to the Giant. "I can't believe we got rid of the bastard so easily. Let us go and tell Mandrill." He threw a sheet from the bed over Urdrill's body, and another over the two halves of the soldier the Giant had slain.

Lalona came back into the room supported by Sonta, and flanked by the other servants. "I'm all right now," she said, but she turned her face away from the bloody mounds.

"Come. We'll escort you to the palace," Dontree said, offering his arm.

Lalona smiled, suddenly shy, and accepted his aid with something close to a blush. Sonta stood back.

Lalona turned to her, and the rest of her servants. "It is over at last," she said. "Clean up my house, and then come to the palace, and ask for me. I love you all."

Outside in the street there came the sounds of cheering and celebration.

Hours later, Mandrill walked into his private sitting room, removing his heavy crown, and throwing off the flowing robes of state. Outside in the square, people still cheered, as they had been cheering their king restored for the past half hour, even though he had left the balcony. He stopped at the small table, and poured himself a glass of wine, and surveyed his guests. The Giant sat in an oversized armchair that had been found somewhere and carted in. It looked out of place amongst the elegant furniture, but then the great size of the giant looked out of place also. Pen sat in a corner, once more nursing his pipe. The Giant, with Dana's help, had diminished his cuts and bruises considerably, and a hot bath and a very good meal had done much to restore him. He stopped the tale of his ordeal at Urdrill's hands as Mandrill entered. Lalona and Dontree sat side by side, each obviously very conscious of the other. Sonta sat on a cushion at Lalona's feet, and looked almost as out of place as the Giant. Mandrill's chief adviser, a wizened little gnome of a man, hurriedly recalled from hiding and still scarcely able to believe his eyes, completed the group.

Mandrill addressed Dontree. "What is this story of an outsider in my son's house?" he asked.

"It is true, My Lord," Dontree said. "The body is downstairs for you to view. It is a woman."

"Elf?"

"No, Lord. An original as far as we can tell. We did not examine it closely."

"Who killed her?"

"It appears she killed herself, Lord. She was alive. My men saw her when they went to take the house. They were fighting their way in, but the house was strongly held. Then when ..." Dontree hesitated, "when proof came that Urdrill was dead -"

"Proof! You mean his head on a pike. You do not have to be delicate with your words, my friend. Remember, he paid the assassin who blinded me, as he told me when he came to gloat on my helplessness. He kept me alive for the pleasure it gave him to see me so. By the Gods of the Firetime! How could my son be so evil?"

"It was not your son, Lord," Dontree said.

"Not my son? Not my son? What mean you? Read me this riddle! Dontree."

"The Giant and Pen here have recognised the outsider woman as an agent of the Red Queen. They say Urdrill was possessed of her. She turned him evil. It is how she works. Another got to Fairein of the Elves, and brought them to ruin."

Mandrill slowly sat down. "This woman killed herself rather than be taken?"

"So it appears, Lord."

"Then she was not held against her will?"

"Not then. No, Lord."

"She once was?"

"So the servants said, when we questioned them."

"Tell me what they said."

"The whole story? Lord?"

"Everything!"

"Urdrill had a patrol out hunting wolves that had attacked the herds. They were not precise as to just when, but before the attack on yourself. They came upon a camp in our lands. About ten men and the woman. No one had been given permission to be in our lands, so Urdrill ordered them killed. The night was hot. The woman was in a tent by herself. She was sleeping on top of her bedding with little, if any, clothing on her body. Urdrill entered, meaning to kill her, but was struck by her beauty, especially the whiteness of her skin and the redness of her hair. Even then, Lord, he was accustomed to enforcing his Princely rights with women. He did not kill the woman but raped her. When all her companions were dead, he allowed the whole hunting party to rape the woman - still meaning to kill her. However, the men asked that she be kept alive until the end of the hunt as they, too, were brought to lust by her strangeness, and wished to enjoy her body as much as possible. It seems Urdrill agreed, and she was tethered in a cave until the next suntime.

"As before, Urdrill was first to enjoy her. They say he spent most of the suntime with her, coming to his powers, again and again, and it was only when he was completely exhausted that he allowed his men a brief time with her. They say Urdrill was so exhausted he could hardly walk. On the third suntime, he did not allow his men access to her at all. When the hunt was over, she was brought in and shut in dungeons controlled by Urdrill's followers. Urdrill used to visit her often. Then he had rooms in his house converted to cells to hold her, and had her brought there. At first they were bare, and she was a prisoner, kept, it seemed, only for the Prince's pleasure. Then Urdrill began furnishing the rooms more and more luxuriously, and his followers noticed that his excesses became more extreme. His character changed. One of his friends tried to tell him that the woman was affecting him. Urdrill had him tortured to death horribly while he and the woman sat naked, side by side, and watched. Then it is said, they drank of his blood and made love upon his body. Then the servants knew that the woman was no longer a prisoner but a terrible mistress in the house, and her every wish was gratified." Dontree fell silent. For a while they all sat enclosed in their own thoughts.

Mandrill stirred. "Tell me of this Red Queen, Pen," he demanded.

The Drark looked up. "It is a long tale, Lord," he warned.

"I have a long time, Pen."

Pen nodded, and slowly began to tell the tale of the capture of Alaine and Dana by the Nasdarks, and his and Fairein's meeting with the Giant.

It was close to waketime by the time his voice fell silent. Mandrill sat motionless. Except for the constant drumming of his finger on the arm of his chair he might have been sleeping. Outside could be heard the voices of the glowlight tenders as they went about watering and feeding the fungus so that the light brightened all over the city. People began to rise as the sun set outside, and workers prepared to move out to tend the crops and herds.

At last Mandrill sighed and stirred. "We have shut ourselves away from the world too long. The Firetime is over, and now the world has come to us, and we, unprepared for it, fell easy victim. That must change. But first one other thing needs urgent solution." He paused and looked at Lalona and Pen, each in turn. "Who is to be heir in my kingdom? The people need an heir unchallengeable or there will be further bloodshed and strife. You, nephew Pen? You, niece Lalona? Each of you are near to my blood. I must choose between you."

Pen blew a thin whirl of smoke from his pipe. "I do not seek your throne, Mandrill. I have learned to love the light of the sun, and the wide strange places of the world. I have companions more dear than life to me, and we have enemy we must destroy, or she will destroy us. I do not wish to sit here as king and wonder each day where, and when, she will strike, and who of my people she is corrupting against me. Name Lalona here your heir. At least a Queen is not subject to seduction by her agents, and it seems she has powers of the mind herself, and may be able to meet this seducer of minds with equal skill. I will be content, but ask only that the home and the lands of my father be returned to me, and enjoy royal stewardship until I return to claim them."

Mandrill gazed at him without speaking for some time. "What would you do?" he asked at last.

"The Red Queen cannot be allowed to live. I would have you loan me fifty picked warriors, those with at least some suneyes to aid the Elves in their struggle with the same forces that ruined your son. Then I would ask that you join with the Elves, and give support to the attack that must be made against the Red Queen, so that she does not yet prevail and bring us all under her sway."

Mandrill turned to Lalona. "Your brother speaks with a fair tongue and a generous one. What say you?"

"I know not what to say, Lord. I, too, have moments when I see this as a dream, and fear to wake up crippled and abused. I have touched the mind of Peter, this Giant, and I have within me memories of deeds heroic and wonderful, and others horrible, of people brave unto death, and good against all odds, and others mean and cowardly and cruel. I have seen, through his eyes, wide lands and fair cities. I have known his joy, and I have known his sorrow. I have glimpsed a love the like I did not know was possible. I think I have within me now that which could make of me a good Queen. I do not know. Only time would tell."

"This touching of minds is a marvel but a danger. Still your words are good. You shall be heir. It will be proclaimed this waking. Pen, you will have what you want, and your name will be forever honoured in this Kingdom. Come, it is time to sleep. We have much to do and need clear heads."

Chapter 7

The Wolf's Throat

"So that is the Dardane. Firetime! But it looks a hard nut to crack!" The Giant stood on a rocky spur overlooking the Dardane valley. About him stood, or sat, fifty Drarks, black bodies in black mail wrapped in black leather against the cold winds. Many of them had thin cloth tied over their eyes to shut out most of the light and allow only a faint glow through.

Pen stood beside him. "Down there." He pointed. "See where the road touches the cliff? That's the Wolf's Throat. That's a harder nut, believe me. But they won't be expecting us from this side, and not in the dark. If we can get down there without being seen, we'll take it, and the Elves will have to change their motto concerning the Wolf's Throat."

"I doubt they'll regret that, Drark. How do you intend to take it?"

"Simple. I think. You contact the Sisterhood in the Stronghold. Get them to organise some sort of diversion to attract the attention of the Nasdarks in the valley. That'll allow us to get down this side unnoticed, I hope. Then you contact Dana, and get the Elves to attack from their side. When they do, I'll go in with half the men. You guard our backs with the other half. If we take the Throat, then you call in the Elves, and we all see what sort of warriors these Nasdarks are."

The Giant nodded. He breathed deeply of the morning air, then relaxed and sat down with his back to the stone of the mountain. His mind sought Dana's. To his surprise, he found her sitting in a tent beside Alaine just outside the Wolf's Throat. About her were the sounds of an armed camp coming to life. "Why are you here?" he demanded, as soon as contact was made. "What has gone wrong?"

"Everything!" Dana made reply. "Fairein is dead by his own hand. He left a note for Alaine. She will not show anyone. All we can get out of her is that he had some sort of dream that convinced him that the Red Queen was able to take over his mind again. He killed himself with his sword. The Elves went into shock. What with the war going so badly, they even had deserters from the arms. No one can remember when that happened last. Alaine took over command of the army even though it might kill her child and herself. I'm sticking close to see if I can prevent that from happening. We have practically the whole army here. The Nasdarks are pressing us, and have us penned against the mountains. Alaine has mounted two attacks against the Throat, but they both failed. We've lost a lot of our best warriors, but if we can't get through, then we've no hope. There are too many Nasdarks to even break out. I don't know where they got so many troops. They must have stripped their land completely bare of men. Did you get the Drarks?"

"Yes. Tell Alaine to hold on until tonight. Then, when I give the word, mount at least a small attack. We'll come in from the Dardane side, and take them from behind. I think we'll be able to do it, but you must survive the day, for without darkness we will have no more success than her warriors did."

"I'll tell her. It will at least give the Elves something to hope for, but this is going to be a long, and terrible, day."

For a few moments Dana and the Giant bonded and enjoyed, and reaffirmed, their love. Then they broke contact, and each turned to the pressing matters in hand. Dana to a troubled day, the Giant to rest after the long night's travel.

Dana turned to Alaine, who sat upon the cushions that formed her bed, and regarded her with a sad smile. "How goes the Giant?" Alaine asked.

Dana looked startled. "How did you know it was he I bonded with? Do I speak aloud?"

Alaine laughed. "No. It is obvious. It is the only time I see you smiling. Has he managed to bring Drarks to clear the throat?"

"Yes. I knew he would manage. The Drarks are now firm allies. But they cannot do anything until it is dark. We've got to hold out until then."

"Can we stall the Nasdarks, think you? We have to hold the front of the Throat, or winning it will do us little good. Otherwise, we could hold up in the valleys, and they would take weeks to shift us. Can you find out from the Sisterhood how many Nasdarks are in the Dardane now? We don't want a force coming through the Throat, and onto out backs when we are fighting."

In a little while, Dana was able to report that there seemed to be only about fifty in the valley, but there were more in the Throat, so probably the total number was about seventy-five. "We'll leave a force of fifty to guard against an attack from them. That should be sufficient. It will prevent them from surprising us anyway. I'll leave one of the women with them, and if anything goes wrong, she can contact you."

Dana nodded. "How are you feeling?" she asked. "Would you like me to check you both out?"

"No. I'm all right. The baby's fine. Let's go out and see to the men. I wish I could put on armour and ride. A leader should be out front, not skulking in a tent behind the lines."

Dana laughed. "A fine sight you'd make, leading a charge. Come on. We might still have to fight for our lives."

The morning was bright and clear. A cold wind poured down off the mountains, but it would soon reverse as the rock walls heated under the early summer sun. The Elfin army came swiftly to arms ready. Horses were already fed and watered, and awaited their riders. Banners of the various arms flicked in the breeze. The First and Second stood to the fore in front of the Throat where they were least protected, and where the main thrust of the attack would surely come. The Fifth were back along the edge of the mountains waiting to reinforce the First and Second. The Third and Fourth, augmented by the remnants of the Eighth and Ninth, which had been severely mauled by the Vipands, guarded the flanks on either side. That was all full strength fighting arms the Elves could muster. Hundreds of their best warriors had been lost in the struggle for the passes when the Nasdarks had first broken through, and hundreds more had fallen to the poison of the Vipands. Behind them, the mountain side was full of a motley crowd of old and young. These were mostly untrained civilians, who were armed with anything they could lay hands on, and who would fight when it became necessary, for only death awaited them if the Nasdarks prevailed. Of the Sixth and Seventh, still apparently holding the south, nothing had been heard. It was feared they were lost, and the Vipands were likely to come down upon them together with the Nasdarks. At the moment they were not in sight, and Alaine hoped that the Nasdarks would be content to wait for them.

It was a hope short-lived however, for it soon became apparent that the foe were readying for a major battle. Row upon row of horsemen took up position in front of spearmen and bowmen. The plan of attack was obvious. The horsemen would hammer into the ranks of the Elves in front of the Throat, and break up their formation. Then the spearmen and bowmen would try to chop their way through to take the Throat. Once that was done, the Elves were lost. The Nasdarks would break through to the Dardane and hold it in force, and the women and children in the stronghold would be doomed.

Alaine set her forces to counter. In front were spearmen and bowmen manning hastily thrown up ramparts of earth and logs. Behind them were the horsemen ready to ride out through gaps to blunt the force of the attack, so that Nasdark horse could not approach the ramparts with sufficient speed to jump them and create a breach.

With the mountains at their back, the Elves would have been confident of holding their foe indefinably, or, at least, until the stocks of food ran out, if they had been facing a like number of foes. However, the Nasdarks were in numbers of at least three to one. They had obviously recruited from the black nations defeated in the wars outside Mandanna. Alaine had begged Fairein to ask the white nations for help, and had thought he had done so. Probably Fairein had meant to do so, but under the influence of the Red Queen he had not, and they could expect no help from there.

Suddenly, a single bugle pealed in the morning air, and the vast line of horsemen moved towards them, gradually building speed. The Elves rode out to meet them, waiting until they were more than half way across the plain, and well in front of their footmen before they gathered speed themselves to strike against them. The result was predictable. The two lines of horse clashed with a sound like the roll of thunder, and all became a turmoil of whirling horses, and flashing blades. The Elves did not try to hold the line, however, but allowed themselves to be pushed back, until they were against the ramparts, where they were let through, and the Nasdarks were met with an unbroken line of spears. Without speed they could not jump the wall, and they merely broke the force of their own foot, who arrived to find horses milling about. Elven bowmen created havoc. There was a brief and bloody battle, and then the Nasdarks' bugles sounded, and they were called back, and reformed. The first round went to the Elves, but there were too many dead or wounded on the field to count it a victory.

Alaine turned to Dana. "What will they do?"

"Narrow down the charge. They'll come arrow formation, heading straight for the Throat."

"What can we do?"

"There is only one thing. Bring the horse in. Send some out to meet them. Others wait to break them up when they get here."

"We are going to run out of horse first."

"Yes. Then we'll just have to do the best we can."

Alaine nodded. "Send the order to the captains."

Dana bent her head and sent. Each captain had an attendant member of the sisterhood. They stopped healing long enough to give the message, and the riders moved in towards the mouth of the Throat. The bugle called again, and the predicted arrow formation formed with deadly efficiency, and rushed at them. They were met with a like arrow, and again the plain became a tangle of fighting horsemen. It was longer, and more deadly. The Elves were not allowed to fall back as they had done previously. Nasdarks broke through in several places, and tried to cut them off. Alaine had to send more and more of her reserves out to clear the path back to the ramparts. Then the Nasdark horse moved sideways along the defences leaving a gap for the spearmen to try to overwhelm the Elves in front of the throat. The Fifth had to be called in, but they prevailed, and once more Nasdarks were recalled and reformed.

They had survived again, but now the gallant horsemen were badly depleted, and the Nasdarks were bringing fresh horse down out of the woods. Alaine looked at Dana. "We can survive one more attack. After that we'll not be able to stop their horse."

Dana nodded. "Then we'll concentrate in front of the Throat, and make a last stand. If we can hang on until night, Giant and the Drarks may be able to let us through into the Dardane. If not, we'll die there."

"As good a place as any. You'll see that I don't get taken alive. I have no wish to be captured again."

Dana grimaced. "Nor I. I'll see that neither of us get taken. It is funny. The Giant once said 'There'll always be knives'. It stopped me from killing myself back at the cave that time."

"Shouldn't you let him know how things stand?"

"No. He'd likely try to fight his way through the Throat. He would get himself killed, and alert the Nasdarks in it. They'd double the guard, and then the Drarks wouldn't be able to clear it. I'll let him know just before I die."

"Here they come again."

The tactic was much the same. But this time, the elfin horses were lured out, and it became obvious that the attack was aimed against them alone. Only few made it back behind the ramparts. The Nasdarks rode off in triumph. The Elves no longer had a viable horse arm. Both sides went out to retrieve their wounded. There were not many Elf wounded. The bodies had mainly been trampled. The Nasdarks reformed. Again, their horse spread right along the line. The ramparts were vulnerable. The whole Nasdark attack line moved slowly forward until it was just some four bow shots away, and then they halted for lunch. They had it like a great picnic, drinking looted Elfin wine, and roasting slaughtered elfin cattle. Alaine ordered her people fed, but those who could stomach the food ate in silence.

The Nasdarks were still eating, and yelling ribald threats as to what they were going to do to the elfin women when the stronghold fell, when a murmur ran through the elfin lines. Dana looked out to see what had caused it. On the edge of the woods, horsemen were moving silently into formation. Strange banners stirred only slightly in the midday stillness. Alaine came to her side. "Is it the Vipands?" she asked.

"It could be. But I think that is the emblem of the Sixth."

"They captured it?"

"I suppose so. But they look too big for Vipands. If it wasn't impossible, I'd say some of them look like Femins. Look, the Nasdarks have seen them.

They're not cheering. They're turning towards them. They're taking defensive positions. It is the Femins! It's got to be! By all that's holy! We're saved!"

"Are you sure?"

"Yes! Yes! See! There's the flag. And it is the Sixth. And the Seventh! By the Firetime, those cursed murderers will not know what hits them."

"Send word for the First and Second to move forward as soon as anyone else moves. We'll hit the bastards from every side, and send any horseman who can still ride. I want Elves in this battle."

Dana stood still long enough to send, and then thrilled when the long thin battle cry of the Femins sheared across the plain, and the lines of horse thundered down upon the Nasdarks. The Elves scrambled over the ramparts to form into spear squadrons, and the horse bounded out through the gaps. The Fifth moved down in front of the throat, as the plain turned into chaos.

Dana and Alaine stood arm in arm cheering themselves hoarse as the battle raged. It was beyond wonder to see the Femins at war. Large and lithe, heavy of horse, and graceful as dancers, they decimated all who stood against them. By their side fought the Elves, and obviously the Kersh and the Bartonians. The Nasdarks had no answer to this onslaught of foes from every side. Their lighter horses were knocked from under them, while blades swung in deadly unison. Arrows streamed in like lethal hail, and elfin spearmen, long pent up behind the barricades, stormed into their ranks.

Even so, the battle lasted all afternoon. There was nowhere for the Nasdarks to go. They closed closer and closer in about their King as more and more died, and then the Femins regrouped. The heaviest horse ploughed into them, splitting them in two, and destroying the king and most of his elite bodyguard. The heart went out of the warriors. One group, composed mainly of foot soldiers, remained to fight. Most of the mounted seized the opportunity when their king died, to cut their way out to the North, and fled the field, closely pursued by Femins. Many died from arrows as they fled. Few would have escaped except for the fact that the Femins had expended most of their arrows in the early part of the battle. The Femins soon returned. Descot, and the rest of the Sixth and Seventh, set off to harry the Nasdarks until the realms of Elfdom were free of them. Deserted by their horsemen, and ringed by grim foes, the remaining Nasdarks fought valiantly on until, at last, exhaustion and wounds took too great a toll, and the survivors threw down their arms and surrendered. It was almost sundown.

Then came the task of healing. Dana and the members of the Sisterhood who had not obeyed Fairein's order to retire to the Dardane, moved down long lines of wounded. Dana did not have the Giant's great strength to draw from, but the Sisterhood, and every past member of it, united to pass that power to those at the scene. Hundreds of warriors were recalled from the very edge of death; thousands, less badly wounded, were relieved of pain and made comfortable, to await attention.

By the early hours of the morning, many of the sisterhood had dropped out, exhausted from their efforts, but then, when the power was becoming too weak to be effective, the Giant suddenly joined Dana. They bonded in love for a few moments, and once again the Sisterhood was bathed in the glory of it, and ecstasy, for a little while, banished weariness and sorrow. Then Dana and the Giant began to work as a team again, and the healing picked up tempo. By mid-morning, the Sisterhood had returned in strength, and there were few still in danger. Dana and the Giant fell into sleep. The Drark sat over them smoking his pipe. And there, Alaine, recently wakened, found him.

"The Throat is clear?" she asked.

He nodded.

"How?"

The Drark reluctantly removed the pipe that he had just got drawing to his satisfaction. "Not difficult. We were waiting for dark when a patrol of Nasdarks blundered into us. They had been sent to Prince Urdrill, who used to rule my people, to get aid he had promised in return for some of your lady captives. We helped them over a cliff, and went down, pretending to be Urdrill's people. When it got dark, I suggested that as we could see so much better, it would be wise for us to take over guarding the throat. The Nasdarks insisted that a couple of their officers accompany us. They died. We guard the Throat, and those Nasdarks who were in the valley are all dead. Your people may come out." He put the pipe back in his mouth and puffed a couple of times. "I couldn't find any of your people to let them know. Most of your officers seem to be amongst the wounded. I thought I'd just wait for the Lady Dana here to wake up. She would know who to tell. I see you have Femins here, too. I would like to meet a certain lady of the Femins again - one Petaine. She is rather a rugged individual, but one I admire a great deal. You know, she threatened to kill me once for calling her a Lady."

"And might still do so, you black Troll!" came a weak but fierce voice from behind them.

They turned to find Petaine glaring with one good eye from out a swath of bandages. The Drark chuckled. "Princess Alaine, may I introduce one of the mightiest warriors of today's world, the Femin Petaine. Call her 'Lady' only while her wounds hold her," he added.

Alaine knelt awkwardly down beside Petaine, and took her hand in both of hers. "Well met, Petaine, how fares your wounds?"

"Well enough, Princess. Your healers do wonders. There is no doubt. Anywhere else, and I would have died, methinks. Fool I was, to let myself be knocked from my horse. The enemy are no more, I presume."

"They were destroyed. The Sixth and Seventh have not returned yet. They will hunt them until there are none left this side of the mountains, and few on the other, if I know Descot."

"True. He is a brave warrior even if he is a man. I wouldn't mind carrying his seed home."

Alaine looked a little shocked. The Drark laughed. "Femins are more frank about such matters, Princess, as Giant and I found on our first visit."

Alaine smiled. "I fear the Elves will have to become so, also, now that we have Dana bonding with the Giant. When ladies bond with men there can be no coyness. You know, the whole Sisterhood dotes on him, second hand as it were. But forgive me. I will have to go and tell Olvar, if I can find him, that the Throat is open. How wonderful this morning compares with last one. I shall come again, Petaine, when I can get away."

"Do not try to do too much, Princess. You are in poor state for hard work."

Alaine laughed and supported her extended belly with both hands. "My little Prince has taken his chances along with the rest of us for the last terrible week. He still kicks vigorously. Today's effort will not harm him, I think." She pushed her way out of the tent as Dana stirred, and rolled over to support her head on the Giant's arm. The Drark smiled. Petaine snorted, but the Drark thought he heard just a tiny bit of envy in the sound.

By mid-morning, most of the Elves were through into the Dardane, and the women and children were streaming down from the Eaglecrest. There was great gladness for their deliverance, but also great sadness for the tragedy of so many young lives lost.

All afternoon the dead of both sides were gathered up and laid out in long rows. The captured Nasdarks were allowed to cremate their dead, while the Elves, and their new allies, held a funeral service for their fallen. There were many despite the heroic efforts of the Sisterhood.

Then Alaine decreed that there should be a great thanksgiving celebration. The stores of food were brought down from the Eaglecrest, and makeshift kitchens were set up all along the Dardane. The Femins, and Kersh, and Bartonians, and Drarks, were feted the long day, and well into the night. Many were the speeches and tales of heroism told, and, if the stories of the deeds of battle grew in valour as the wine dwindled, who cared? All were in mood to cheer truth or fable with equal vigour. And if the euphoria and the wine, led to indiscretions, and unexpected conceptions, then few cared about that either.

Next morning, with aching heads, the elfin families gathered their belongings and their children, and started the long trek to their homes. Alaine called a council of the allies, at which the activities of the Red Queen were explained, and the Giant told of the Firetime weapon that must now be in her possession. It was decided that a Great Council should be convened for the first day of spring the following year to which the leaders of all friendly nations would be invited, to plan war against the Red Queen. To that end, all were asked to seek her out, and make ready a strike force commensurate with the size of their population.

Chapter 8

Respite

The Femins, Kersh, and Bartonians had left. The Nasdarks prisoners had been stripped of their weapons, and had been sent home carrying the dead body of their king. Had they had sufficient forces, the Elves might have reclaimed the lands to the Sharn once more, but they had lost too many warriors, and it would take years to rebuild strength. Alaine's last appeal to the Elves as they left for their homes was to bear babies to repopulate the lands.

The mourning, and the celebrations, were over. Fairein had been laid to rest with all the trappings of royalty. Almost unnoticed in the turmoil, his father, too, had passed away. He, too, was interred with due pomp and ceremony. The Elves set about rebuilding their shattered lives.

Alaine called a conference of all the heads of leading families, and royal advisors. The great conference room of the palace filled to capacity, and Dana and Alaine stood on a balcony overlooking the crowd. They consisted mainly of the very old and the very young. So many of the middle-aged heads of families had perished, it looked almost as though one complete generation was missing.

Alaine sighed. "I hope this goes well," she whispered as she allowed Dana to aid her descend the stairs, and take her seat at the head of the table. She sat in the chair formally used by Fairein. The chair beside her was empty.

She sat still for some minutes while the chatter and shuffling slowly died down. Then she rose ponderously to her feet. "I bid you welcome," she said into the sudden silence. "As you know, we have gathered to name a successor to my late husband, Fairein, who would now have been King."

She stood looking across the heads of the crowd as the murmuring built up, and then faded away. All waited on her next words. "We live in strange, and dangerous, times. We have a foe who would destroy us...one who is embittered to the edge of madness. A foe who uses corruption and possession of minds to achieve her ends. So she corrupted, and eventually possessed, the mind of my husband through her agent Wolverina. You all knew the girl, or knew of her. When we knew her, she was a completely untaught child. When she was with Fairein she was the Red Queen herself, and, as the Red Queen, she seduced and corrupted my husband. In this, I, and the mid-wives who attended me, must bear some of the blame. Because of this, no mid-wife shall attend me until the child is being born. The Lady Dana will be my companion, and will see to my needs. That is one change that will occur. The other is more serious, and will need the concurrence of the majority of you. I inherited my husband's mantle in time of need, and no one denied me. I intend, with your permission, to continue to wear it."

She held up a hand imperiously as voices rose in dissent. Again, she waited until the noise abated. "I do not propose this lightly, and I do not do it to seek power, but to preserve the integrity of the elfin nation. This conflict was brought about because the Nasdark King, and the Kings of the Black nations, were dominated by the Red Queen, through her agents - women. It so nearly succeeded because the Prince of the Drarks, and the Prince of the

Elves, were corrupted by the Red Queen through her agents - women. I propose that, as a woman, I should rule, at least until the Red Queen is no more. I will be least likely to be vulnerable to the wiles of this foe, and the Lady Dana who, of you all, has done most to defeat her will aid me. To this end, I propose to name a Regent to aid me in my task, until my child, if it be male, is of an age to inherit."

"This is very irregular, Princess," one aged advisor protested. "This regent is not to be your husband?"

"No. I will not marry for the convenience of the state. Nor do I want the relationship between myself and the regent to be complicated by the laws of marriage. If any deny me the right of ascendancy to be your Queen, let him or her, speak now."

There was considerable murmuring but no individual raised his voice against her.

"So let it be. I know it is not traditional for a Queen to reign in our nations, but there is a Queen reigning as our foe, and I believe that a nation with a Queen is safer from her. If any amongst you believe this false, let him speak now."

One of the few middle-aged Elves pushed through to the front.

"Canton, of Bower Hill," murmured Dana to Alaine. "He could cause trouble. He has a distant claim to the throne."

"I do not agree, Princess, that a King is more at risk now, than a Queen. We are now warned, and know what to expect. Surely no King now would fall in the same snare as Prince Fairein did."

"If you know what to expect, good Canton, then you might be good enough to inform us all. It is hardly likely that the Red Queen will use the same trap. Will you inform us what one she will use?" She suddenly looked up and swept the whole room. "And she will use one. Remember, we, the Elfin women, alone have the mind power to defeat her. She wants us dead, all of us. She very nearly succeeded. If the Lady Dana and her friends had not befriended and influenced our recent allies to come to our aid, who amongst you has any doubt that we would have been defeated outside the Wolf's Throat, and our women and children would now be facing death? It was the purest luck for our nation that we have been saved. Do you want to add anything to the risk when next we face the Red Queen?"

At this, a rumble of voices rose in agreement, and Canton, reading the mood of the assembly, bowed, and retired into the anonymity of the crowd.

"Who would you name Regent, Princess?" a tall old man asked.

Alaine hesitated. "I have thought long on this. He, who is close to the throne, and who led our warriors valiantly in our great struggle for survival, and who is obviously fit to continue the struggle against the foe; he, I have chosen. I put his name to you. He is Fairein's cousin Descot."

Again, there rose a rumble of voices, argument rippled across the room, and back again. Alaine waited, her gravid body still as a marble statue in the chair, only her eyes flashed with life following the flow of voices, noting the dissenters, and those who argued against them. Dana stood behind her chair, equally still, but serving as a reminder that these two women had led the Elves to salvation when their Prince had failed his people. At last, the dissenters found a spokesman, and Tanoi of the Darkenfield Valley moved to the fore.

"There are many of us, Princess, who feel that times of trouble are not the times we should break with the traditions that have stood our nation in good stead since the Firetime. We would name a new King."

Alaine nodded. "Who would you have rule before me, Tanoi?" she asked pleasantly.

Tanoi flushed. "Obviously, Princess, one would have to be chosen. It is not for I to say who that should be."

Alaine's voice rose slightly, and took on an imperious edge. "Do you mean to say, that you would support any before me, so long as he be male?" Her voice rose higher to encompass the whole room. "Which man amongst you could have led better than I in our hour of peril? And tell us what you would have changed."

There was an embarrassed shuffling, and Tanoi found his supporters fading away from him. Suddenly, he experienced the sensation that he was standing entirely alone, and that he was the focus of every eye in the room. The eyes that concerned him most, however, were those of his Princess, soon, apparently, to be Queen and unopposed ruler of the nation, and he had a very uncomfortable feeling that she was committing his face and name to memory. He hurriedly bowed low. "I meant no criticism of yourself, and your leadership, Princess," he hurried to assure her. "It is tradition alone I would seek to defend." He looked round, trying to catch the eye of a supporter, but none appeared to even recognise him. With another deep bow, and an almost audible curse, he stepped back into the crowd that opened for him, and allowed him far more space than others had.

Alaine took quick advantage of the situation. "If there are others who would like to speak, please do so now."

No one else had sufficient faith in their supporters to risk her wrath, and so the room remained silent. Alaine let the silence linger for about two minutes, and then spoke. "Then it shall be as I have spoken. I would have Descot asked to attend my advisers and me in my rooms." She rose awkwardly, and Dana moved quickly to aid her. The movement reminded the watchers how difficult the preceding days must have been for her, and someone in the crowd cheered, another took up the cry, and suddenly it seemed that the whole room was alive with applause.

The news spread quickly through the streets, and Descot, hurrying in from where he had been working with Olvar, trying to reorganise the depleted strike forces, was perplexed to find grand citizens bowing low as they made way for him.

✳✳✳

It was the night after the coronation. Celebrations could still be heard faintly in the City. Alaine's time was very close. She rested on cushions, exhausted from the hours of ceremony. As always, Dana sat beside her. The Giant sat on a chair especially crafted for him. The Drark sat by the window gazing out into the night, where the stars shone over the rooftops, and the faint outlines of distant mountains could be seen against the horizon. Descot sat uncomfortably straight, not yet accustomed to his new status and responsibilities. His wife Byanna perched shyly beside Dana, still obviously overwhelmed by her rise to royalty.

Alaine sighed. "I'll be glad when the baby is born. It must be a boy, he kicks so much. I'm sure I did not abuse my mother so."

Dana laughed. "You probably did. I don't suppose she'd complain to you about it. But never mind. I wouldn't be surprised if it comes this night. Make certain you rest. You've had a hard day, and it will not be good if you are exhausted before the labour starts."

"Yes. I'll retire soon. I can hardly keep my eyes open. But before I go, I would know your plans, Giant, and yours, too, Drark. Will you stay with us, and help us against the Red Queen come next spring?"

The Giant smiled. "I will be happy to, Your Highness, though it seems to me that we should spend the time in seeking her out rather than sitting still. What say you, Drark?"

Dana spoke before the Drark could answer. "I have a good idea where she is, or at least the direction in which she lives," she said.

"How so?" the Giant asked surprised that recent bonding had not revealed information of such importance.

"When we ambushed her in the mind of Fairein, I clung to her, and followed her homewards. She fought me, and then she realised that I was tracking her, and she broke the connection, but I feel I was very near her when she did."

The Giant showed even greater surprise. "But we have bonded often since then, and I did not know."

Dana smiled indulgently. "When we have bonded you have had other things on your mind, Peter."

The Giant coloured, and grinned sheepishly. The Drark laughed deeply. Alaine looked slightly envious, and Descot and Byanna merely looked puzzled.

"Where is she?" Alaine asked.

"In the mountains, west of the Vipands - where we suspected all along. There's a pass in the mountains - that's where I lost her."

"Then that is where we'll seek her, Firetime weapon or no. What forces do we have, Descot?"

"We have only four full strike forces, Your Highness. We are recruiting as many as possible, but we'll have to let the men home to get the harvests in. That will curtail training."

"I know. We lost too many people. But I have nightmares thinking how much worse it would have been, if you three had not gone south when you did, and we hadn't got help from those wonderful Femins. Weren't they magnificent? I warrant those Nasdarks will treat women with a bit more respect after this. Help me, Dana. I'm going to bed. Good night to you all. But, Drark... I'm sorry, Pen, you did not say if you will stay with us, or will you now return to your home."

"I may go home for a short time, your Highness, but I will return. My people, too, have an account to settle with the Red Queen. There will be Drarks with your forces, I promise."

"And welcomed they will be, Pen. We have had little opportunity to show our gratitude for the opening of the Wolf's Throat, but the Elves will never forget it."

Pen only smiled his cat's smile, and bowed deeply, as she and Dana left the room. "And what now, Giant?" he asked.

"To bed and to sleep, Drark." He yawned widely. "The battle's won, but the war is not."

If you enjoyed this author's book, then please place a review up at the site of purchase, and any social media sites you frequent!

You can find ALL our books up on our website at:

https://www.writers-exchange.com

All Dan's Books:

https://www.writers-exchange.com/Dan-Donoghue/

All our Science Fiction Novels:

https://www.writers-exchange.com/category/genres/science-fiction-time-travel/

All our Young Adult Novels:

https://www.writers-exchange.com/category/genres/young-adult/

About the Author

Dan Donoghue grew up in country Queensland, receiving his primary education in small one-teacher schools and completing his secondary education at boarding school in Cairns. He went on to gain a Bachelor of Education degree at the University of Queensland, and spent many years teaching English in Queensland schools. He began writing novels as a progression from his love of reading, and as a form of stress management. He has always been fascinated by the possibility of mind powers beyond the norm and much of his writing reflects this. Most of his working life was with young adults and as he believes that the later teens can be the most exciting and formative time in a person's life it is of those he loves to write.

You can keep track of all his books on his author page:

https://www.writers-exchange.com/Dan-Donoghue/

If you want to read more about books by this author, they are listed on the following pages...

Alien Thought

{Science Fiction}

An ordinary Saturday morning turns extraordinary for seventeen-year-old Dave Duggan when a couple of girls from his school ask for help in finding their way into the mountains beyond their town. At first the jaunt is uneventful but holds the promise of adventure and possibly romance.

After entering a dark area of rainforest, birds, bugs and small animals inexplicably begin to die around them. Dave's life is threatened and no reasonable explanation fits. Only far sinister possibilities make sense. Forced to take responsibility for three lives, Dave finds himself losing his heart while in very real danger of losing his life.

Publisher: https://www.writers-exchange.com/alien-thought/

Dead by the Sea

{Murder Mystery}

When a brutal murder occurs on the beach where he's staying, Jim Groggan's bored enough to start checking things out for himself. He even agrees to drive a police officer down along the beach to interview Hippies in a seaside camp.

There he meets a girl he finds himself aiding even when it means getting mixed up with drugs, guns, and murder. Suddenly, boredom seemed a very desirable state to be in...

Publisher: https://www.writers-exchange.com/dead-by-the-sea/

Red Queen Series

{Fantasy: Dystopian Post-Apocalyptic}

Set in a post-nuclear Medieval world, civilisation has reverted to Feudalism, complicated by societies of mutants developed after the radiation stemming from the Firetime wars. Each remnant clan jealously guards their racial purity and homelands with incessant squabbling. Into this tumultuous and unstable situation comes the influence of the Red Queen, a mutant with unimaginably strong mind powers. Able to possess, control and corrupt minds at a distance, she uses beautiful, young female agents to seduce those in power that stand in the way of her ruthless quest for absolute dominion.

Book 1: Red Queen Dawning

The Red Queen has brought a formidable weapon from the past into the present in order to instigate a war. A photograph is discovered that gives credence to the lies of one race and effectively pits nation against nation.

In the south is a mythical island that has been rumoured to have escaped the direct ravages of the nuclear war. Three diverse mutant outcasts agree to travel to this island to discover if the weapon is real, what it is and whether there's anything that can counter it.

Giant, an outcast rejected because of his impure lineage, searches for meaning in his life by undertaking the quest. He helps rescue an Elfin Princess and Dana, her personal guard and healer.

Dana, having been raped by Nasdarks captors, is an outcast because she's considered unclean by her people. Also joining the group is Drark, another outcast from a nation of cave dwellers, with powerful night vision. As a mutant, he sees much but says little.

Together, the group face the dangers of journeying through the lands of warring nations, encounter religious fanatics as well as the reputably impassable "Fire-Time Sands" to discover just what the relic is and how to neutralise it before their civilisation is ripped apart.

Publisher: https://www.writers-exchange.com/red-queen-dawning/

Book 2: Strike of the Viper

The Red Queen has gained control of the King of the Nasdarks by employing the snake worshipping, poison-wielding Vipand warriors she's corrupted and controls. Now she's set her sights on destroying the Elf Nation. Her first task is to send out one of her agents to try to seduce and corrupt the prince of the elves.

Giant, Dana and Drark, mutant outcasts, continue their struggle against the Red Queen and attempt to save the Elves. In order to succeed, they must locate the holocaust weapon the enemy of their world intends to use to return Firetime nuclear warfare to their already shattered land.

Publisher: https://www.writers-exchange.com/strike-of-the-viper/

Sensitive

{Science Fiction}

In a galaxy overwrought with unrest and war, one exceptionally-bred Sensitive is called upon to save them all from interplanetary war...

Wolf Carthar was reared in a primitive tribal environment on Earth. He is an extremely powerful Sensitive who can shield his mind against invasion by other Sensitives. Isolated by nature, framed and exiled for love, he is sent to a planet discovered and settled by Americans.

High America suffers one severe drawback to development: For reasons yet unknown, Sensitives are unable to survive on it. With the odds stacked against him right from the beginning, Wolf struggles to clear the planet of invaders and make it possible to survive.

He must discover and defeat the source of death on High America--the killing machine--that lures Sensitives like him to their deaths...or fall victim to its power himself.

Publisher: https://www.writers-exchange.com/sensitive/